"You've never been in love?"

Julia cocked her head as she stared at him, waiting for an answer.

He leaned toward her and lowered his voice. "I've been in lust, Julia, more than once. And when I was young, I thought it was love. But time proved me wrong."

"I—I'm sorry, Nick."

Her unwanted sympathy irritated him. "I don't need you to feel sorry for me, Julia. I'm fine the way I am. And if you think love is so important, why aren't you married?" He was very interested in her answer.

"You can't just decide to fall in love." She shrugged. "I hope to fall in love one day. It just hasn't happened yet."

He saw the longing in her eyes, heard it in her voice and he felt a response in himself. One that scared the hell out of him.

Dear Reader,

No month better suits Silhouette Romance than February. For it celebrates that breathless feeling of first love, the priceless experiences and memories that come with a longtime love and the many hopes and dreams that give a couple's life together so much meaning. At Silhouette Romance, our writers try to capture all these feelings in their timeless tales…and this month's lineup is no exception.

Our PERPETUALLY YOURS promotion continues this month with a charming tale from Sandra Paul. In *Domesticating Luc* (#1802) a dog trainer gets more than she bargained for when she takes on an unruly puppy and his very obstinate and irresistible owner. Beloved author Judy Christenberry returns to the lineup with *Honeymoon Hunt* (#1803)—a madcap adventure in which two opposites pair up to find their parents who have eloped, but instead wind up on a tight race to the finish line, er, altar! In *A Dash of Romance* (#1804) Elizabeth Harbison creates the perfect recipe for love when she pairs a self-made billionaire with a spirited waitress. Cathie Linz rounds out the offerings with *Lone Star Marine* (#1805). Part of her MEN OF HONOR series, this poignant romance features a wounded soldier who craves only the solitude to heal, and finds that his lively and beautiful neighbor just might be the key to the future he hadn't dreamed possible.

As always, be sure to return next month when Alice Sharpe concludes our PERPETUALLY YOURS promotion.

Happy reading.

Ann Leslie Tuttle
Associate Senior Editor

Please address questions and book requests to:
Silhouette Reader Service
U.S.: 3010 Walden Ave., P.O. Box 1325, Buffalo, NY 14269
Canadian: P.O. Box 609, Fort Erie, Ont. L2A 5X3

JUDY
Christenberry

THE
HONEYMOON
HUNT

SILHOUETTE *Romance*®

Published by Silhouette Books

America's Publisher of Contemporary Romance

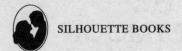 SILHOUETTE BOOKS

ISBN 0-373-19803-5

HONEYMOON HUNT

Copyright © 2006 by Judy Russell Christenberry

Visit Silhouette Books at www.eHarlequin.com

Printed in U.S.A.

Books by Judy Christenberry

Silhouette Romance

The Nine-Month Bride #1324
*Marry Me, Kate #1344
*Baby in Her Arms #1350
*A Ring for Cinderella #1356
†Never Let You Go #1453
†The Borrowed Groom #1457
†Cherish the Boss #1463
**Snowbound Sweetheart #1476
Newborn Daddy #1511
When the Lights Went Out... #1547
**Least Likely To Wed #1570
Daddy on the Doorstep #1654
**Beauty & the Beastly Rancher #1678
**The Last Crawford Bachelor #1715
Finding a Family #1762
††The Texan's Reluctant Bride #1778
††The Texan's Tiny Dilemma #1782
††The Texan's Suite Romance #1787
Honeymoon Hunt #1803

*The Lucky Charm Sisters
†The Circle K Sisters
**From the Circle K
††Lone Star Brides

Silhouette Books

The Coltons
The Doctor Delivers

A Colton Family Christmas
"The Diplomat's Daughter"

Lone Star Country Club
The Last Bachelor

JUDY CHRISTENBERRY

has been writing romances for over fifteen years because she loves happy endings as much as her readers do. She's a bestselling author for Harlequin American Romance, but she has a long love of traditional romances and is delighted to tell a story that brings those elements to the reader. A former high school French teacher, Judy devotes her time to writing. She hopes readers have as much fun reading her stories as she does writing them. She spends her spare time reading, watching her favorite sports teams and keeping track of her two adult daughters.

Chapter One

Julia Chance drove slowly down the block in her rental car, anxiously looking from one side of the street to the other, growing more and more uneasy as she went.

She was looking for the Hotel Luna. She was sure she'd followed directions, but she couldn't imagine her mother being in this neighborhood.

Old, run-down buildings crowded each other in this area of Dallas. Minimarts, aglow with their bright interior lights, battled with the dark bars that found residence on at least every other street. Men loitered in dark alleys between the buildings, prompting her to step on the gas and keep moving.

There on the right, a couple hundred feet up, a small sign drew her attention. Hotel L*na. Despite the sign's missing letter, Julia knew that had to be it.

She drove up to the hotel and pulled to the curb, but hesitated. The hotel looked anything but safe. Surely her mother wouldn't—

From inside the Hotel Luna a man came running, startling her. He was big, muscular, wearing a white knit shirt from what she could see in the dim street-light. Maybe he was running because he was in a hurry, or maybe he—

Just then, the passenger door was opened, cutting off her thought, and the man she'd glimpsed earlier jumped into her car.

"Step on it, lady!" he ordered with a growl.

Julia's eyes widened in surprise. Almost as a re-flex, she resisted. "I'll do no such thing! Get out of my car or I'll call the police!"

She heard a sound similar to a loud pop right be-fore her windshield split. As it happened, the man be-side her grabbed Julia and yanked her down.

"What's going on? Who's shooting at you?"

"I accidentally interrupted a drug deal," the man growled.

It took a minute for her to put things together. By that time, another bullet had hit her windshield. Then pain from her right foot shot through her as the man did as he'd asked her to do.

He stepped on the gas pedal, pushing it to the floor-board, ignoring the fact that her foot was under his.

He also grabbed the wheel, rising up just enough to see over the hood.

Julia felt like a coward, but she couldn't bring herself to sit up and face any more bullets. Who was shooting? It could be the police, for all she knew. Was the man in her car the target? This guy could be a criminal escaping.

Well, he'd carjacked the wrong woman! She straightened and tried to wrest the steering wheel from his grasp. "Take your hands off. I'm the driver!"

To her surprise, he released the wheel. "Then drive. Get on the freeway. The entrance is right here."

"What if I don't want to get on the freeway?"

"Then we'll both be killed! You don't have much choice."

The sound of a car behind them had her looking in the rearview mirror, but she couldn't see much.

"They're after us!" Again he slammed his foot on hers to increase their speed.

"I'm going to call the police if you don't get out right now!"

"Do you have a phone? I seem to have lost mine. But call the police! I'd be more than happy to see a black-and-white."

"You would?" Julia asked, surprised by his answer. *Surely he must be a bad guy,* she thought.

"Yeah, but hurry. They're closing in on us quickly."

"Who? Who is—"

She ended her questioning as bullets began to fly in their direction again. This time, she raced for the freeway, actually running a red light as she noted there was no traffic coming. She'd never done such an outrageous thing in her life!

They shot onto the freeway—and were immediately pulled over by a police car.

"Oh, dear! I don't know—"

"Let me handle it!" the carjacker/passenger snapped.

The officer knocked on the glass and waited for Julia to lower the window.

Then he said, "You folks have an emergency, or do you just ignore posted speed limits?"

"Yes, officer, we do have an emergency," the stranger beside her said calmly. Even his body language spoke of ease, but Julia was shaking.

"As you can see, we've run into trouble," he said, gesturing to the bullet holes in the windshield.

"Where were you when this happened?" the officer asked, studying the evidence.

"We were looking for the Hotel Luna on Westmoreland," the man said, causing Julia to look at him sharply. He was going to the hotel, too? She eyed him up and down, taking in his neatly trimmed brown hair, white shirt and pressed slacks. Not exactly Hotel Luna clientele, she thought.

The cop shook his head. "Not a good neighborhood."

"We discovered that."

"Can you tell me who shot at you?"

The stranger shrugged. "Couldn't tell you. We must've just been in the wrong place at the wrong time."

"All right. If you'll both come to my patrol car, I need to take a report. Either of you hurt? Do you need an ambulance?"

Both men looked at Julia, but she shook her head.

"No, we're both fine. Just a little shocked," the man answered.

"Then come with me." The cop opened Julia's door and escorted her back to his patrol car. He put her in the back seat while the man got in the front passenger seat.

First, the policeman used his radio to send some squad cars to the Hotel Luna. Then he took a clipboard and asked the man for his name.

Julia leaned forward, interested in that information herself.

Instead of speaking out loud, the man reached into his coat pocket and pulled out a business card.

"Thank you…" The cop read his name. "Mr. Rampling. And is this your wife?"

"No! No, she's not."

Julia leaned forward and gave her name and home address in Houston.

"So you're both from out of town? Where are you staying?"

Julia immediately supplied the name of the hotel where she was staying, including the street address. She frowned when Mr. Rampling just nodded. Was he staying there, too? It was way too coincidental for her.

Before she could protest, the policeman went on to their reason for being at the Hotel Luna. Again, she waited for his answer, wondering if her surmise was correct.

"We were looking for our parents. They told us they would be at that hotel, but they've led us on a wild-goose chase," the man said, a sad expression on his face.

How did he know she was looking for her mother? And that her mother was with a man—apparently this Mr. Rampling's father? How was it that he had all the details she was missing? She didn't know the identity of her mother's partner, only his first name.

And why was the young Mr. Rampling searching for his father?

At least, she thought, he wasn't a carjacker.

The cop made some further notations, then said, "Okay, that about sums it up. If you'll call before you leave town, we'll let you know if we've found anything."

Mr. Rampling extended his hand. "Thanks for your help."

"No problem." The officer turned to her. "Remember to follow the speed limit, ma'am. You don't want to cause an accident."

"Thank you," Julia added, feeling she should express her appreciation, too.

"No problem, ma'am." He put on his hat and helped her out to escort her back to her car.

Once behind the wheel, Julia closed her eyes and drew a deep breath.

"You okay?"

She glared at him. "Yes, no thanks to you!"

"Hey, would you have preferred to stay down there and get shot?" he demanded, irritated by her response.

"No, but—"

"But nothing! I did what I had to do. Now, let's get going."

"Going where?"

"To your hotel."

"*My* hotel?" She stared at him, confused and shocked at his suggestion. Apparently young Mr. Rampling had lied to the officer. He wasn't staying at the hotel, after all. But now he expected her to be hospitable. "You can't be serious! You jump in my car, get me shot at, pulled over by a policeman, and you expect me to take you to my hotel? I don't think so!"

"Look, lady, I just need to use a phone and have a safe place to wait until I get some help. I don't think that's asking too much."

"Well, I do!" When he didn't leave her car instantly, she said, "I'd have to be pretty stupid to do as you've suggested. You'd probably try to lure me into bed!"

"You have nothing to worry about there. You're not my type!"

"What a relief! And that's supposed to make me feel safe? Get out!"

"Take me to a phone before you throw me out. That's the least you can do since I saved your life."

He had a point. Not one she liked, but she couldn't disagree with him. Of course, he was the reason they'd been shot at, but he had pulled her down and gotten them out of that place.

And most important of all, he had information she needed.

Driving down the freeway, she tried to sound casual as she asked, "Your father said he would be at the Hotel Luna?"

"Yeah."

"And you assumed that's why I was there, too?"

"Of course I did. Your mother is with my father. We both know that, so there's no need to pretend any longer."

"I'm not pretending anything. I'm here to find my mother!"

"So I figured. Why else would you be down in that neighborhood?"

Silence.

"How did you get there?" she finally asked.

"By taxi. The driver promised to wait, but must've driven away as soon as I was inside."

"That was rather naive of you, wasn't it?" she asked, feeling superior.

"Not if you knew what I'd paid him." His voice sounded grim.

"Where are you from?" she asked.

"I'm from Kansas City." After a pause, he asked, "Does your mother usually hang out in dives?"

Julia snapped her head around to frown sternly at him. "Of course not!"

"Well, it couldn't have been my father's idea. How did you find out about the Hotel Luna?"

"She wrote me and…told me she was staying at the Hotel Luna in Dallas."

"My father wrote me the same thing."

"So it could be your father who hangs out in dives."

"No way!"

She gave him a hard stare and almost drove off the road.

He grabbed the wheel. "Pay attention to your driving!"

"Sorry," she muttered. "Why are you so sure it wasn't your father?"

"Doesn't matter."

"Were you worried about him meeting my mom?"

"No! I was worried about him shacking up with your mom."

"How dare you! My mother would not do such a thing!"

"Then what made you come after her?"

Julia didn't want to answer that question. Instead, she pulled off at the next exit. As soon as she saw a gas station with a phone booth on the corner, she pulled in. "Get out. There's a phone booth. Make your calls and stay away from me and my mother!"

"Gladly, as long as you and your mother stay away from my father!"

She told herself she was relieved when he opened the door and got out of her car. She didn't hesitate to drive away. But she watched him in her rearview mirror all the way back to the freeway.

Nick Rampling stared after the woman. She hadn't seemed like the daughter of a schemer, but women had lied before. Especially to men with money. God knew, he'd tried to protect his father, but it hadn't been easy.

What was he going to do now?

Pulling himself together, he headed for the phone booth. After tapping in the numbers of his calling card, he waited until he got an answer.

"Hello?" a groggy voice said.

"Mike, it's Nick. I need your help."

"Uh, sure, Nick. What can I do?"

"Do you have something to write with?"

"Just a minute."

In the background, Nick could hear an irritated woman's voice, sure it was Patti, his vice president's wife. Mike assured her that nothing was wrong, that it was just Nick calling.

Nick did occasionally interrupt his people's private lives, but he paid them well for the inconvenience.

"Okay, Nick, I'm ready."

"My father wasn't where he said he'd be. I think it was an obvious attempt to delay my finding him. Find out if he's used his credit cards and where. And get Browning on the job. I want a full report in the morning. I'll be at the—" He leaned out the telephone booth and then turned back to the phone. "I'll be at the Motel 6 on Central Expressway in Dallas. Have him call me there."

"The Motel 6?" Mike asked in astonishment.

"It's the nearest hotel, and I don't have any cash to get a taxi." That afternoon he'd run off after his father in such a rush, he hadn't stopped for cash. Nor had he thought of it. "I'll need you to send some money to me. I doubt there's a cash machine in the lobby."

"Yes, sir. I'll take care of everything," Mike crisply agreed.

Nick suspected his right-hand man found it amusing that his boss was sleeping at an economy motel when he owned a dozen hotels renowned for their elegance. But Nick could manage for one night; he'd spent worse nights elsewhere.

The walk to the motel was short, but it gave him time to think about the young woman who'd just dropped him off. She had more spunk than he'd expected. At first, he'd thought she was an innocent who'd lost her way, till she told the cop her name.

Throughout the ordeal she'd never seemed jolted until he'd criticized her mother. Then she'd dumped him like a bag of trash. Unlike her mother, she must not know how much money he and his father had.

Or maybe she was playing the innocent. He'd been burned a few times by women who looked like one thing but were actually another.

He entered the motel and requested a room for the night.

"All right, sir. How did you want to pay for the room?" the clerk asked.

Nick pulled out his American Express card. "Will this do?"

The clerk relaxed. "Yes, of course. Do you have some ID?"

Nick showed his driver's license.

The clerk examined it and visually matched the photo with Nick. He handed it back with an apology. "We have to be so careful these days."

"Yeah," Nick agreed. Wasn't that the truth?

* * *

Julia tossed and turned all night, until finally morning dawned. She still had no idea where her mother was. If she was safe…and happy. A couple of days ago, Lois Chance had written a brief note telling Julia she wasn't coming home to Houston as planned because she'd met Abe, who had persuaded her to stop off in Dallas. There was no last name, no other indication who Abe was.

Her mother had gone on a "summer in New York" tour with her best friend, Evelyn. AARP had offered the trip and promised it would be safe. Julia had approved her mother's decision to go, feeling Lois had spent much too long mourning her husband's death two years ago.

But there was a big difference in going on a trip with a female friend and deciding to make a stopover with an unknown man. After all, her mother was an innocent. An innocent with the proceeds from her husband's insurance policy that was to provide for her financially for the rest of her life.

Moments after she'd read the note, it had occurred to Julia that her mother might have revealed that piece of financial information to Abe. As much as she didn't want to think her mother might be deceived, Julia feared that had happened. Especially when she'd seen the Hotel Luna.

What should she do now?

Lying under the covers, she tried to think about her choices. She could call Evelyn and see if she'd heard from her mother. But she didn't think—

Pounding on her door interrupted her thoughts.

Who could that be? She hurried out of bed and put on her robe. Then she tiptoed to the door and looked through the peephole.

With a gasp, she backed away from the door.

"Miss Chance? Are you in there?"

The voice had haunted her most of the night. It was Abe's son, the one who had accused her mother of "shacking up" with his father.

Julia stood there for a moment, debating her choices. Then she reached for the knob. "Yes, I'm here, Mr. Rampling," she said as she opened the door.

He looked at her from head to toe. "Sorry to wake you up. I supposed you'd be out looking for your mother."

"I don't know where to look. Do you?"

"Not yet, but I will. I have a few questions to ask you before I head out."

"Head out where?"

He raised his eyebrows, which drew her attention to his remarkable blue eyes. In the darkness last night, she hadn't been able to see them. "I'm the one looking for answers, Miss Chance."

"No, Mr. Rampling, we're both looking for answers. You just think you hold all the cards. But I'm not that gullible. I'll answer your questions if you share your information with me."

"You don't have a bargaining chip in this search, Miss Chance. I can manage without information from you."

Julia crossed her arms over her chest. "If that were true, Mr. Rampling, you wouldn't be here."

"Look, Miss Chance—"

"Oh, for heavens sake, call me Julia."

"Okay, fine, Julia. I can get by without your information. But it might speed up the process if you'll answer a few questions. In return, I promise to bring your mother back to you as soon as possible."

"Not good enough, Mr. Rampling. I want to protect my mother, to make sure she's not hurt. So either we share information or I tell you nothing."

"Forget it. I'll manage on my own." He turned around and started walking away.

Julia dashed out past him so she could face him. "I won't let you walk away. I'll follow you."

He gave her a leering grin. "In your nightgown? That should be interesting."

Julia had forgotten she wasn't dressed...or packed. It would take her at least half an hour to take care of those details, and she knew the man wouldn't wait.

She felt her cheeks heating up and gathered the collar of her robe, pulling it closer together.

Suddenly he had a change of heart, one she didn't understand. But she wasn't going to argue about it.

"Meet me for lunch at the Mansion on Turtle Creek," he said. "We'll see what we can work out."

"Where is the Mansion?"

He rolled those sparkling blue eyes. "It's one of the most famous hotels in the world. Take a taxi. The driver will find it for you. One hour. If you're not there, I'll go on alone. Understand?"

"I understand, and I'll be there," she assured him. Wherever it was.

He gave her a sharp nod and walked around her down the hallway.

Julia hurried into her room to start packing. She only paused to dress. She didn't bother to put on makeup. The man had already seen her with her face scrubbed clean. The important thing was her mother. She had to find out what had happened to her mother.

And his name. She'd like to know her new partner's name, too.

Chapter Two

The maître d' didn't raise his eyebrows at her slacks and blouse as Julia walked into the stately mansion that was an elegant restaurant attached to the hotel by the same name. But he was a little surprised by her suitcase.

"Welcome to the Mansion, Miss. May I take your...suitcase for you?"

Julia let out a sigh. "Thank you so much. I turned in my rental car, and I didn't have a place to leave it."

"We'll keep it safe until after you've dined. Will it be lunch for one?"

"Oh, no, I'm meeting Mr. Rampling for lunch."

Instantly the man's manner became respectful. "Right this way, Miss Chance. Mr. Rampling is waiting."

He led the way into a second room that looked as if it had once been a library.

Julia joined him, trying to look at everything at once. She wasn't prepared to see Mr. Rampling just yet. But there he was, waiting for her.

The maître d' pulled out her chair and handed her a menu. "Your waiter will be right with you."

"Hello," Julia said to the man across from her.

"I'm glad you made it, Julia," he said.

Her eyebrows rose. "You thought I'd give up on my own mother?"

"She's with my father, you know, not some Mob guy." He seemed affronted by her comments.

"I have only your word for his character," she told him. She knew nothing of Abe Rampling. Or his son, for that matter.

Apparently, though, he was a mind reader.

"My father and I are in the hotel business, Julia."

"Oh. Well, that doesn't mean you aren't connected to the Mob."

"I think you watch too much television." He glanced at the menu. "Have you chosen what you want?"

"No, I— It will just take a minute." She opened her menu and sucked in air. The prices were discreetly printed on the menu, but that didn't make them any easier to swallow.

As soon as she closed the menu, the waiter appeared at the table. Julia said, "I'll have the tortilla soup."

"Of course, madam. And the entrée?"

"No, that's all."

Though he looked surprised, he turned to Mr. Rampling. "And you, sir?"

"I'll have the tortilla soup also. Then I want the sirloin cut with a broccoli side."

"Yes, sir. How would you like that cooked?"

"Medium-well." He looked at Julia. "Are you sure you won't join me for a steak?"

"No, thank you. Oh, and we'll need separate checks, please."

The waiter appeared startled and looked at her dining companion.

"That won't be necessary," he said quietly.

Before Julia could protest, the waiter hurried away.

"Why did you do that?" she demanded.

"For the sake of my reputation," he assured her with a smile.

"I couldn't care less about your reputation!"

"Then feel free to leave," he said softly.

Julia snapped her lips together. She couldn't do that until she found out what he knew.

"Very well," she said stiffly. "I'll pay you after we leave here."

With heavy sarcasm, he replied, "I think I can handle the price of a bowl of soup."

"That's not necessary. I pay my own way."

"And what do you do for a living, Julia?"

She hesitated, chewing on her bottom lip.

"Come now, I've already told you what I do."

"I'm a teacher," she finally said.

He frowned. "Is that why you only ordered soup?"

"No! I—I just wasn't hungry."

"I'm willing to buy you lunch so I can get the information I need."

"I have another price in mind," she muttered. "Look, Mr.— You never told me your first name."

"And that matters?"

She drew in another deep breath. "I thought we'd agreed to swap information."

He looked at her as if he were testing her mettle. Then he said simply, "Nick."

"Very well, Nick. I think we can share our information and be more efficient."

"I'll certainly be more efficient. But I don't see the need for you to be efficient."

"I want to find my mother as much as you want to find your father."

"Why? My father is a great catch. I'm not surprised your mother trapped him."

Julia drew back, anger filling her. "My mother never set out to seduce your father. She's never done that!"

"You don't know that."

His matter-of-fact tone made her crazy. "Yes, I do," she snapped.

Nick leaned in closer, as if letting her in on a secret. "Look, Julia, my father loves women. Your mother's not the first one who thought it would be easy to latch onto our fortune."

Fortune...? As if a lightbulb had lit up over her head, Julia realized he was Nick Rampling of the

Rampling Hotels. She remembered reading about him recently. Wealthy, successful and a real catch, judging by the eye candy constantly photographed on his arm. His father had retired some years ago, leaving Nick to run the family business, worth hundreds of millions.

But Nick wasn't the focus of their talk; her mother was.

Mustering an attitude, she replied, "My mother doesn't need your money!"

"Independently wealthy, is she?"

Certainly not on the Rampling scale, she thought. But Lois Chance was comfortably well off.

The waiter's arrival gave her a reprieve from having to answer.

The waiter carefully placed each bowl in front of them. "Enjoy," he murmured as he withdrew.

"I believe they're famous for this particular soup," Nick said.

"It's quite good," Julia said politely, as if she were attending a social tea.

"Are your parents divorced?" Nick asked after spoonful.

"No. My father died two years ago."

She was afraid he would say something offensive. Holding on to her temper, she waited for his response.

All he said was, "I'm sorry."

She looked up, shocked by his sensitivity.

"Why do you look so surprised? You think I can't sympathize?"

"I'm sorry," she hurriedly apologized.

"That doesn't make me any happier that your mother latched onto my father, but at least she's not bitter."

She should have known, Julia thought. She'd obviously been suckered by Nick. "I take back my apology!"

"No need to be difficult, Julia."

"No need to be insulting, Nick."

He smiled. "All right, now we can get down to business."

She stared at him, not sure exactly what he meant.

"Has your mother dated much since she became a widow?"

"Of course not. That's why—" She stopped abruptly.

"That's why what?" Nick asked, staring at her.

Julia lifted her chin. "That's why I encouraged her to go on the trip. She had mourned too long."

"So you sent her off to find a new man?"

"Absolutely not! I—I encouraged her to go on a tour to New York. She needed to start enjoying life again."

"With my father?"

"I didn't know your father and you know it! I thought she'd go to a few shows and do some shopping with her friend Evelyn."

"So you don't know your mother as well as you thought, do you?"

"I know my mother. I *don't* know your father!" Nor did she know his son. But what she saw, she didn't like.

The waiter returned to collect their plates and serve Nick his meal.

"Can I get you anything else?"

"Yes, bring the lady some crème brûlée, please, so she'll have something to eat."

"No, I—"

Nick waved the waiter away. "Quit protesting. Their crème brûlée is even better than the tortilla soup."

She sat there stiffly, promising herself she wouldn't touch the crème brûlée no matter how good it was.

A few minutes later, the waiter returned with a crème brûlée topped with raspberry sauce. Her mouth watered as she stared at it.

"Come on, Julia," he said with a saccharine voice, his eyes nearly twinkling as he turned on the charm, "eat the dessert. It will make you sweet."

"It will do no such thing!"

"Eat it anyway. I can't send it back."

Julia debated the wisdom of giving in, but she finally picked up her spoon and tasted it.

"I told you it was good," Nick said with a smile.

Julia put down her spoon. It was very good. But she was irritated with herself for having given him a reason to think he'd beaten her.

When she didn't take another bite, Nick frowned. "Come on, Julia, I wasn't trying to make you feel bad. Besides, I'll feel bad if I eat a big meal and you don't eat anything else. Really."

"All right, I'll eat it. But we need to discuss what we're going to do."

"We?"

"That's right," Julia said firmly.

"It was my understanding that we would exchange information, but that was all."

"I told you I had another idea. I want to go with you to find them. I don't think you're going to be very nice to my mother and I want to be sure she's okay." She didn't think her mother would be strong enough to deal with the loss of another man she loved. The last couple of years had been difficult for Lois, and dealing with Nick Rampling would only make things more difficult.

"I promise to deliver her to your very doorstep. Satisfied?"

"No, I'm not. I'm not concerned with her physical well-being. I'm concerned with her emotional well-being."

"You can deal with that after I bring her home."

Julia put down her spoon. "I can't agree to that."

He mimicked her, putting down his fork. "Lady, you're acting like you're in control. You're not!" His finger punctuated his remark.

She pointed right back at him. "Neither are you! I agreed to answer your questions as long as you shared your information with me. So far, I've done my part. When do you fulfill your part of the bargain?"

He opened his mouth to deny her accusation. Then he suddenly shut it again.

"Well?" she prompted.

"You're right. I haven't given you any information. But I'm not going to have any until one-thirty. That's when my investigator is going to call me and tell me what he's found out."

Julia stared at him. "You hired an investigator?" She frowned as if he'd told her something scandalous.

"He's on my payroll. We have to have one for the hotels. So I thought he could help me out here, too."

"Does your father know you would turn the investigator loose on him?"

"Probably."

"So it's your fault they sent us on a wild-goose chase!"

"I'm not one of your students who broke a rule, Julia." His eyes narrowed as he observed her. "What grade do you teach?"

"That doesn't matter!" she exclaimed. She didn't want to tell him she taught the second grade. He'd think that she was sweet and nice, and that he could walk all over her. That had happened to her before. This time, though, she was going to stand up for herself and her mother.

"Yes, it does. Well?"

"Second grade," she admitted, her chin going up, as it always did when she was being stubborn.

"Ah," he said and smiled.

Julia glared at him. "Don't think you can discount me because I teach young children!"

He didn't address her remark, merely took the last bite of his meal. When he'd swallowed, he said, "Finish your dessert. We need to leave for the airport."

Julia folded her napkin and put it beside her plate. "I'm ready."

"Don't you want to finish that?" he asked, staring at her dessert, only half-eaten.

"No, I'm ready to go hear the latest information you have."

The waiter returned to their table and offered coffee, but Nick turned it down and asked for the check.

Julia opened her purse, having figured out how much her lunch had cost, and took out enough cash to cover it, plus a tip. Once they were in a taxi she would give it to Nick. She knew he'd try to embarrass her in the restaurant to have his way.

When the waiter brought the check, Nick asked him to call a cab for them. He paid the bill in cash, leaving a healthy tip. Then he pulled her chair back for her to stand and join him.

"Is it one-thirty yet?" she asked.

"No, but it will be when we get to the airport. I'm sure there'll be a flight home to Houston that you can take."

Home? Julia opened her mouth, but then thought better and closed it. Home was one place she wasn't going. Still, she'd save that argument until it was necessary.

Nick escorted her to the waiting taxi, stopping to pick up her suitcase and his.

Once the cab had started for the airport, Julia handed him the portion of the lunch tab.

"What's this?" he demanded with a frown.

"The cost of my lunch," she explained calmly.

"Damn it, take it back before I put you out of this cab right now!" he exclaimed.

His threat didn't intimidate her. "So you have no intention of keeping your word?" she retorted.

He seethed in silence for several minutes while the taxi driver watched him in the rearview mirror.

When he opened his mouth, he spoke calmly. "Julia, I said I would pay for lunch. There's no need for you to do so."

"But I believe I told you I pay my own way, Nick Rampling. I see no reason to change now. Especially when you suspect my mother of trying to steal your money!"

"I see no need to nickel-and-dime you."

"Since I prefer to handle my own expenses, I expect you to honor that decision." She dumped the cash in his lap and turned to look out the window.

"Is your mother as stubborn as you?" he asked, exasperation in his tone.

"No, absolutely not. She told me I got my stubbornness from my father." She didn't tell him that she knew her mother was lying. That was none of his business!

Nick couldn't believe he'd been bested by a grade-school teacher. He'd intended to get a little information from her, pat her on her head and send her home. Now he realized it wasn't going to be that simple. She'd managed to outmaneuver him with her virginal blush and innocent blue eyes, topped by her beautiful long blond hair.

Not that he cared what she looked like.

Nor did he care that she was a virgin—or so he thought. She looked way too sweet and innocent to be experienced. No, she'd just taken him by surprise, that was all.

When they reached the airport, he paid off the taxi and was grateful she didn't insist on counting out her share in one-dollar bills right there in the street. He escorted her inside and pulled out the new cell phone he'd picked up that morning, along with a suitcase and clothes. "If you'll excuse me, I'll phone my investigator to see what he's found out."

"Is your cell a speakerphone?"

He answered truthfully before he thought. "Yes, of course."

"Good. So I can hear the conversation, too."

"I'd rather the rest of the world didn't hear, if you don't mind."

"Let's go back outside. I don't remember hordes of people out there."

He glared at her, but he finally moved toward the door.

Once they were outside the terminal, Julia seated herself on one half of a stone bench and waited.

Nick stood their suitcases next to the bench and sat down as he took out his cell phone. He dialed the number for his investigator.

"Browning? This is Nick. I'm putting you on speakerphone." He wanted the man to know someone was listening besides himself.

"Nick? Why am I on speakerphone?" Pat Browning asked.

"I'm with Mrs. Chance's daughter, Julia. We joined forces here in Dallas."

"Oh. Well, they're several days ahead of you. They left Dallas three days ago and flew to L.A. They're staying at your hotel there."

"They're still there?" he asked in surprise.

"The hotel thinks so. None of the staff wanted to go find out. Apparently Abe told them not to worry about waiting on them. They would manage on their own. And there's a Do Not Disturb sign on the door."

"All right, thanks, Pat. *I'll* be on the next plane to L.A. and I'll disturb them when I get there."

"Okay, boss. Let me know if you need anything else."

Nick hung up the phone and started to head back into the terminal.

"Where are you going?" Julia's cool voice asked, reminding Nick of his companion.

"Uh, I'm going to L.A. I'll bring your mother back to you."

"No, thank you. I'm going to accompany you, if you don't mind."

"That's really not—"

"Necessary? I think it is."

He conceded on this one. Anything to get going. "Fine. Come on. I'll get the reservations on the phone and then we can pick up the tickets at the counter."

"All right," she agreed, following him into the building. He had both their bags.

Nick announced that he'd reserved their seats.

But when they arrived at the ticket desk, they ran into a slight problem.

Julia took out her credit card and said she would pay for her own ticket. But when the woman announced the price of the tickets, Julia almost passed out. "Why does it cost so much?" she demanded.

"That's the normal price for first class, ma'am."

"First class? I don't want first class. Please put me in coach."

"I'm sorry. Coach is sold out. I can give you a reservation in coach on the red-eye. It leaves at eleven o'clock tonight."

Nick watched as Julia stood there, trying to figure out what to do. He started to offer to buy her ticket, but she made her decision before he could.

"No, I'll take the first-class seat." She pushed her card across the desk.

"Are you sure you don't want me to pay for your ticket?" he leaned forward and said softly.

She shook her head and said nothing. In fact, she didn't speak until they were seated and the plane was pulling away from the gate.

"How long will the flight take?" she finally asked.

"Three hours."

"Shouldn't we have called them first to be sure they were there?" Julia asked.

"No," Nick said. "If we let them know we've found them, they'd be gone by the time we got there."

"Why would they do that?"

"If they're married, they know I'm going to have

it annulled. And if they're not married, they'll know you're going to be upset."

"Why would you have it annulled? If they're in love—"

"Dad falls in love every other week or so. And your mother probably fell in love with his money, not him." His father was gullible when it came to beautiful women. After his second marriage had failed, he'd looked for love over and over again. Nick felt it was his duty to protect his father, but the job was becoming impossible.

"My mother is not like that!" Julia protested as the plane took off.

"So you say."

"Why are you so cynical?" she demanded.

"Because I'm not a second-grade teacher, honey. It's just not in me."

A beautiful red-haired flight attendant halted what would no doubt have been a stinging retort. "Good afternoon. May I serve you a drink?"

"Yes, I'd like a Diet Coke, please," Julia said.

"Certainly. And you, sir?"

"I'd like a bottle of water, please."

The redhead smiled and batted her lashes several times at Nick. He returned the smile before he picked up the in-flight magazine.

Julia watched him out of the corner of her eye. He seemed quite at ease. She supposed he flew often. She didn't know where his other hotels were, but if he had a hotel in Los Angeles, he would have to fly to the west coast frequently.

Maybe he even knew the friendly flight attendant.

The woman returned with their drinks and placed Nick's on his tray.

Julia had assumed the tray was on the back of the seat in front of her. But it wasn't there.

"Ma'am, if you'll bring up your tray, I'll set the drink on it."

Julia didn't want to acknowledge that she had no idea how to find her tray.

It was Nick who came to her aid. He reached over and pulled her tray up.

"Thank you."

She sounded embarrassed. The flight attendant's smug look didn't help any, Nick guessed. He fought the protective instinct that suddenly arose in him. He hadn't expected to have any feelings for Julia at all. But her determination to protect her mother and to pay her own way had touched him.

"Are we going to be served a meal of any kind?" he asked the redhead.

"We'll be serving a meal in an hour. But if you're hungry, I can bring you something now, Mr. Rampling."

He turned to Julia. "Honey, do you want a snack now, or can you wait?"

"I can wait," Julia responded.

He looked at the flight attendant, who wasn't as warm and friendly to him as she had been earlier. "I believe we'll wait for the meal, but thanks for the offer."

"Yes, sir. Let me know if you need anything."

He nodded and she hurried away.

"Thank you for finding my tray."

Her quiet words drew his attention. "When you haven't traveled first class before, you wouldn't know."

A few minutes later, after finishing her Diet Coke, she turned to look out the window.

Nick smiled. He'd guessed she'd prefer the window seat. However, after a few minutes when she hadn't moved, he realized she was asleep.

She must not have slept well last night. He leaned over and pushed the button to lower the back of her seat as far as it would go.

The flight attendant immediately appeared. "Would your wife like a pillow, Mr. Rampling?"

Chapter Three

The question took him by surprise. Not the pillow part, but the wife part. "She's not my wife," he whispered fiercely.

"I beg your pardon, sir. Would your…companion like a pillow?"

Her suddenly smug look irritated him. "Yes!" he snapped.

When she brought him the pillow, he leaned over and slipped it between Julia and the window. He needed to get rid of that protective feeling he had. Julia certainly hadn't asked for his assistance. In fact, she had seemed determined to pay her own way. An unusual occurrence in his life. The women he dated always expected him to pay. Not only for food and transportation, but also for expensive gifts.

Of course, he wasn't dating Julia.

A light snore from his companion interrupted his thoughts. He wondered if anyone had ever told her she snored. Somehow, he didn't think so. He couldn't picture Julia Chance with a lover. She appeared too…too untouched. When he found himself taking inventory of Julia's slender beauty, he shook his head. He had to stop thinking about Julia Chance.

He wanted nothing to do with her.

Julia's eyes fluttered open and she stared around her, not sure why she was on a plane. Until her gaze collided with the broad-shouldered man next to her. Nick Rampling.

She straightened up, worried her sleeping might have made her look weak. Around Nick, she had to be careful about how she came off. After all, he was obviously a man of the world, experienced in all things.

All things…

She wasn't experienced in *that* way, either. Not that Nick would ever find out. She'd gotten engaged in college and her fiancé had tried to force her into bed with him. But she'd resisted and had broken off the engagement.

When she felt Nick moving beside her, she stretched. "I'm sorry. Did I miss anything?"

"No. You must not have slept well last night."

Julia looked away. "No, I was worried about my mother."

"Are you worried about whether she'll appreciate your concern?"

"No. I know she'll appreciate it."

"Trust me, Julia, I can tell you from experience, your mother will not want your interference. My father never does."

Julia gathered her courage. "You make it sound as if he elopes every week."

"Not quite that often." Nick shrugged. "But I'll admit this is the first time he's ever chosen an older woman. However, if your mother looks anything like you, I'm not surprised."

"I suppose you think I should be flattered, Nick, but I'm not. In order to marry her, a man should feel more than admiration for a woman's looks. Looks fade. Her soul is always there."

"And you think my father is in love with your mother's soul? Right." He looked as if he were about to laugh.

"Yes, I do, because my mother wouldn't marry a man just because he flatters her."

Her chin was in the air. She was not going to allow him to destroy what her mother must be feeling now. That was the very reason she was along on the trip to Los Angeles.

Turning toward the window, she ignored Nick. His opinion of his father's behavior wasn't encouraging. But she was relying on her mother's behavior. She knew her mother would not be with Abe Rampling if she didn't believe that she loved him…and that he loved her.

At fifty-two, Lois Chance was young enough to start a new life, but still old-fashioned enough to not sleep around with strange men interested only in a fling. She was a levelheaded woman who would have to have a good reason to do something impetuous.

The flight attendant brought warm, damp towels, much to Julia's surprise. She watched Nick clean his hands with the towel, so she did the same and found it delightfully refreshing. The redhead took back the towels and returned with small cups of warm nuts.

They were Julia's favorite. As she ate them, she looked over her shoulder and discovered that the door to the coach section was closed. "Are we the only ones receiving the towelettes and the nuts?"

"Yeah. They've got to give us some reason for paying the higher prices," Nick said with a grin. When she stopped eating, he asked, "What's wrong. Don't you like them?"

"Yes, I do," Julia said. "But don't you feel bad eating in front of the others?"

He looked around with a frown. "Who? They're all eating their nuts."

"But not the passengers in coach," she pointed out.

"Damn it, Julia, they don't care about warm nuts if they get cheaper airfare!"

Julia nodded and ate another nut. But the difference in coach and first class still bothered her. "Are they being served anything?"

"They get a snack!" Nick snapped at her as if he'd had enough.

Why did he always seem to get irritated whenever she asked anything?

She stopped asking questions, stopped talking altogether.

When the meal was served, she ate her baked chicken in silence.

After a moment, Nick said, "Are you pouting?"

Julia looked up in surprise. "Why would you think that?"

He glared at her. "You stopped asking those ridiculous questions."

"I don't think concern for others is ridiculous. But it was obvious I was irritating you, so I stopped." She took another bite of chicken and stared at the seat in front of her.

"Just like that? Because you figure out you're irritating me?"

"Is that a problem?" she asked stiffly.

He stared at her before he said, "No. Not a problem. And I'm sorry I was so…impatient with you. I'm not used to having my lifestyle questioned."

"I didn't mean— Obviously I owe you an apology, too. It wasn't my intention to make you uncomfortable. But our lifestyles, as you put it, *are* quite different."

She was still avoiding his gaze. She almost jumped out of her seat when his warm hand settled on her arm. "W-What?"

He withdrew his hand at once. "I was trying to apologize," he said.

"Not necessary. We have a deal. That's all there

is between us. I'm trying to make it as painless as it can be for both of us."

Her response irritated Nick even more. What made her so perfect? She didn't think they had anything personal going on? Why did she think he had let her come along? He could've managed without the information from her. True, he thought it might help to keep her mother under control if he had her along. But he could've managed just fine on his own!

She couldn't be real, anyway. No woman worried about those less fortunate than herself when she was flying first class. At least, no woman he'd ever been with.

He figured she was putting on a show to convince him her mother wasn't after their money. But she could give that up. He knew better than to buy her act.

When the flight attendant came to remove their meal trays, Nick realized Julia hadn't finished. "Didn't you like your lunch?"

"Yes, I did."

"Then why did you let her take your tray before you'd finished?"

She drew a deep breath. "I didn't want to cause trouble."

He closed his eyes, then opened them to stare at Julia. "Honey, you paid for first class. You can tell her to leave your tray until you finish."

She shrugged. "Now I'll have room for dessert,"

she said, a smile on her lips. "Believe me, Nick, I would've kept it if I'd been starving. But I'm not."

The dessert was worth it, a rich chocolate cake drizzled with bittersweet chocolate sauce and topped with raspberries.

Julia didn't hesitate to dig in.

"Now you can have two desserts," Nick told her. "I don't really want mine."

Julia looked at him. "No, thank you. It's very good. You should try some."

Disgruntled, Nick picked up his fork and took a bite. He didn't really want the dessert, but he was miffed that Julia had turned him down. Once he tasted the dessert, he decided to eat it.

"How much longer until we reach L.A.?" Julia asked as she put down her fork.

"We've been in flight a little over two hours... It should be about forty-five minutes," Nick said. "You looking forward to seeing your mother?"

"Yes, I am. Aren't you looking forward to seeing your father?"

"Not really. He's going to be upset when he sees me."

"Because he knows you don't believe him?"

He frowned. "Why should I?"

"Because he's your father."

"But he doesn't love any of them. He's easily convinced. When I face the woman, she's willing to be bought off."

"I see," Julia said slowly.

"So I guess your mother is going to come into

some extra money very soon. Do you want to nego-
tiate the amount now so we'll have that out of the
way when we get there?"

Julia was appalled by his audacity. But she com-
posed her features and politely said, "No, thank you."

"That's it? 'No, thank you'?"

She half stood and moved toward him, saying,
"Excuse me."

He rose and stepped into the aisle to allow her to
get out. He assumed she was going to the bathroom,
so he leaned down and whispered, "They're up
front."

She ignored him and headed to the back of the
plane.

He frowned after her and sat back down. A few
minutes later, he waved to the flight attendant.

"My companion went to the back of the plane. I
think she may have gotten confused. Could you
check on her?"

"Of course, Mr. Rampling."

Nick sat there wondering if he'd misunderstood
what she was doing. Or had she gotten disoriented
or become ill?

The redhead returned almost at once. "Mr. Rampling, I informed her you were concerned. She said
to tell you to go to…sleep. Apparently she just wants
to stretch her legs."

Nick thanked the redhead. Then his knuckles
tightened. Julia Chance was driving him crazy. One
moment, he felt he needed to protect her; the next,
he wanted to yell at her.

Now, she'd completely walked away from him. But she'd have to return to get off the plane!

Julia remained in the back of the plane for the rest of the flight, talking to a couple of the crew. When the seat belt sign came on, she finally returned. Without saying anything, she slid into her seat.

"Where have you been?" Nick demanded, anger in his voice.

"Stretching my legs," she said calmly.

"For that long?" he demanded.

"For as long as I want, Nick. I didn't promise to entertain you. I promised to take care of my mother."

He folded his arms over his chest and stared straight ahead. "Right."

Obviously, she'd offended him. But his feelings weren't her responsibility. He certainly wasn't concerned with her mother's feelings. Or his father's, either, for that matter.

When the plane landed, Julia silently followed Nick off the plane after he had collected their two small bags. She hoped she would be on a plane that night, perhaps with her mother, on the way home to Houston. She didn't have any clean clothes left. She'd just packed one change of clothes for her short trip to Dallas. Somehow, that seemed to have happened a long time ago.

She expected Nick to summon a taxi, but instead he opened the door of a limousine for her.

"Don't you think this is a little extravagant?" she asked.

Nick cocked an eyebrow at her. "This limousine

belongs to our hotel. They pick up any important vis-
itors."

"I don't think I'm an important visitor," Julia said
hesitantly.

"No, but *I* am," he said briskly and waved her into
the limousine.

Once he'd joined her inside, the chauffeur closed
the door and got behind the wheel.

"Would the limo pick up your dad, too?" Julia
suddenly asked.

"Yes, of course."

She leaned forward and knocked on the glass that
separated them from the chauffeur.

Fortunately, the man had not pulled away from the
sidewalk. He rolled down the glass. "Yes, ma'am?"

"Did you pick up Abe Rampling and my mother
about three days ago?"

"I picked up Mr. Rampling and a guest then, yes."

"Did she look like me, only older and with shorter
hair?"

The man nodded. "Yeah, come to think of it, she
did."

"Were they happy?" Julia asked softly.

"That doesn't matter!" Nick said at once.

"Yes, it does. Were they?" Julia asked again.

"Yes, ma'am. It seemed like it to me. They were
laughing a lot."

"Oh, thank you," Julia said.

"Did they use the limo at any other times?" Nick
asked.

"No, sir. Someone at the hotel said she thought

they were on their honeymoon because they'd gone
to the suite and hadn't come out."

"They must still be there," Julia said, crossing her
fingers.

"Don't count on it," Nick muttered.

She glared at him as the limo pulled away from
the curb.

They spent the thirty-minute ride in silence. Julia
was hoping her mother was still there, happily married. She knew Nick wasn't hoping the same thing.
He didn't want them married no matter what.

A beautiful woman in a dove-gray suit met them
at the door of the elegant Rampling hotel. "Mr.
Rampling! Welcome. How may I serve you?"

Julia stared at the woman. She was practically
salivating at the prospect of "serving" Nick. No wonder he was spoiled.

"I'm here to see my father. Have you seen him
since he checked in?"

"No, sir," she said with a chuckle. "He and his
companion told us they didn't need any service."
She looked at Nick and seemed to be surprised by
his annoyed reaction. Her smile faded. "Shall I call
him?" she asked hesitantly.

"No, we'll go up." He turned away without saying anything else.

Julia noted the woman's sudden fear. "Thank
you," she said softly and smiled.

The woman replied hurriedly, "Let me know if I
can do anything."

"Yes, we will," Julia assured her. Then she caught up with Nick, waiting impatiently by the elevator.

"What were you saying to her?" he demanded.

"I said thank-you—which is what you should've said."

He glared at her, then nodded. "Okay, you're right. But I was thinking about Dad."

The elevator door opened and Nick gestured for her to enter ahead of him. When she got in, he followed.

"Don't we need a key to get to the penthouse?" she asked.

"I have it," he said and he inserted the key card into the elevator pad.

She didn't ask anything else as the elevator shot up twenty floors. But excitement was building in her.

When the elevator door opened, they emerged into an elegantly decorated hallway with a double door in front of them.

Her heart was pounding as they approached the door and knocked.

But no one answered.

After a minute, when there still had been no response, Nick opened the door with a master. The place looked as if it hadn't been touched. Julia stepped in, but it was obvious the penthouse wasn't occupied. Nick headed for one of the closed doors. Then he opened two others.

"Any sign of them?" Julia asked, though she knew her disappointment sounded in her voice.

"No. I don't think they spent even one night here."

"Then where are they?"

"I don't know." He let out a disgusted breath. "I'll call Pat again. I should've kept him working the case. I knew Dad would hide from me."

"I think your family has a strange relationship."

"You act as if I don't love my father. I can assure you I do. But he has to be protected!"

What kind of strange dynamic operated between the two of them, she wondered. "I think—"

"Don't tell me what you think. We obviously don't agree and I'm too tired to argue!" He ran a hand through his dark hair, leaving it ruffled and sexy.

He crossed to the sofa and picked up the phone. After dialing a lot of numbers, he got Pat Browning.

"It's Nick. They're not here, Pat…. No. No signs that they even stayed here. You got any ideas?"

After a minute he added, "Yeah, I should've thought of that. We'll head there in the morning."

When he hung up the phone, Julia asked, "Where are we going in the morning?"

"Pat pointed out that if they were looking to get married fast, they probably went to Vegas, knowing I'd come here first since they had shown up here so publicly."

"Ah. Of course." After thinking for a moment, she asked, "We can't go this evening?"

"No, it'll be better to get a good night's sleep and go in the morning," he said, certain he was right.

"I see. Well, I'll go get a room and see you in the morning." She stood and started for the elevator.

"Don't be ridiculous!"

Julia turned to stare at him. "I beg your pardon?"

"We have three bedrooms here, Julia. How many do you need?"

"I—I don't think—"

"You have your choice. I'll take one of the other two, okay? I'll have dinner sent up in a little while. You can take a nap if you want."

She gave him an exasperated look. "No, I can't. I have to go shopping for some clean clothes."

"Don't worry. I'll have the shop downstairs send up some things. What size are you?" he asked as he reached for the phone.

"Stop! I can't afford the clothes from your shop. They'll be outrageously expensive."

He frowned. "How do you know that?"

She shook her head. "Because I've looked in hotel shops before."

"Okay, I'll tell them to put them on my account."

"Now *you're* being ridiculous. The rumors you'd start would be numerous. And I really don't want to be talked about that way." She picked up her purse and headed for the door again.

"Wait! I'll go with you."

She turned around slowly. "Why would you do that? You'll just be bored."

"Because I don't think you'll be coming back here tonight if I don't keep an eye on you."

Her cheeks burned and she dropped her gaze.

"See? I was right."

"I intended to return to the hotel," she insisted.

"Yeah, but you weren't going to stay up here. You were going to waste your money on a hotel room you don't need."

"I don't think it's a good idea to stay here with you."

"No one will even know. Let's go find some stores."

Julia drew a deep breath. Before she could think of any more protests, Nick grabbed her arm and headed for the elevator.

When they reached the lobby, he walked to the front desk. "Is the limo free?"

"Of course, Mr. Rampling," one of the clerks said.

"Good." He looked at the people on duty. Then he said, "Miss Wilson? I need to ask you a question."

The young woman hurried over and Nick asked quietly, "Where are the best shopping areas?"

The young woman stood straighter. "Well, sir, Rodeo Drive is the best, of course, but Neiman Marcus is not too far away, and I believe there's a Saks Fifth Avenue close to it, too."

"Great, thanks," he said with a nod. Then he turned and headed for the front door, still holding on to Julia's arm.

The chauffeur was waiting by the back door of the limo. As soon as he saw them, he swung the door open.

Julia slid into the limo, watching Nick tell the driver where he wanted to go. He joined her with a smug look on his face.

As soon as the driver got in, Julia did as she had

the last time she'd wanted to talk to him. She knocked on the glass.

Immediately, he rolled down the window. "Yes, ma'am?"

"Where did Mr. Rampling tell you to take us?"

"He suggested we go to Rodeo Drive and then Neiman Marcus."

"See?" Nick pointed out. "I told him exactly what Miss Wilson told me."

"That's nice. Too bad you didn't ask her to join you, because I have no need to visit those stores."

Both men stared at her, looking confused.

"You said you wanted to go shopping!" Nick exclaimed.

"Yes, but I need to shop where I can afford to buy something." She looked at the driver. "Can you take me to a Target, please?"

Chapter Four

"Target?" Nick exploded. "Why Target?"

"Because I can get what I need and still be able to buy a meal or two. On Rodeo Drive, I could buy one blouse for a fortune and not look any better when I wear it!"

"I could—"

Julia spun around in the seat and glared at him. "Don't say it. Just don't say it."

"But, Julia—"

"No! The moment I take help from you, I'll be just like all the other women you despise, including my mother. I won't do that to her or me."

From the front seat came a quiet voice. "Sir, shall I—"

"Drive to Target," Nick agreed wearily.

Satisfied with herself, Julia sat back. "You should've stayed at the hotel and taken a nap. You didn't sleep on the plane like I did."

Nick rolled his eyes. "I think I'm tired from doing battle with you!" Life with Julia seemed much more difficult than with any other woman. But more interesting, too.

He shook his head. He didn't know where that stray thought had come from.

"What are you upset about now?"

"I didn't say anything!" he protested.

"You were shaking your head," Julia insisted.

"I was just thinking about…things. How far is it, James?"

"A few minutes, sir."

Good. He only had to withstand minutes in this limo with her.

"We're here, sir," the chauffeur said as he turned into a large parking lot.

Nick frowned. "Take us to the door and then park where you can see us when we come out."

Before the chauffeur could respond, Julia protested again. "Us? *You* can wait in the limo. I won't take that long."

The chauffeur looked in the rearview mirror for his employer's response.

"Do as I said, James," Nick ordered, ignoring Julia's objection.

Before she could get out a coherent protest, he explained to her, "I can't let you go in there alone, Julia. I'm responsible for your being here."

"You're being silly. There's no danger in going into Target by myself."

"Then just call me nosy. I want to see what kind of bargains you can buy in this store." After all, he was an expert on the price of women's clothing. At least, if the shopping was done at Neiman's or on Rodeo Drive. Many of the women he'd dated had wanted him to bankroll a shopping expedition. But he didn't want to mention that to Julia.

With a sigh, Julia sat back, her arms crossed over her chest in disgust, waiting until they reached the front door where she, along with Nick, would be allowed to exit the limo.

When they entered Target, Nick couldn't believe the crowds and the selections. It seemed anything one wanted could be found in the big store.

Julia looked over her shoulder and then reached back to grab Nick by the arm. "If you don't want to get lost, keep up," she ordered crisply.

She hurried to casual wear and picked out three tops. She added two pairs of jeans. Then she headed to the dressing rooms. "Wait here," she ordered again.

Nick didn't see that he had much choice. But it gave him time to think about their shopping expedition. His first thought was how totally different it was from any other he'd been on. And not just because he wouldn't be asked to foot the bill.

His second thought was disappointment, because he didn't think Julia would come out and model for his benefit. He thought he might have enjoyed that.

That reminded him—she'd need something besides jeans. He should encourage her to at least buy one skirt.

She came out of the dressing room a few minutes later.

"How did they fit?"

"Fine," she returned and continued walking.

Nick moved faster to keep up with her. "I thought I should mention that you may need a skirt in Vegas."

She gave him a sharp look. "Why?"

"Some places have a dress code," he muttered. He hoped she'd never been to Vegas or she'd know better.

She looked disgusted. "Nice try," she said with sarcasm.

Again she walked off without him. But he caught up—just as she got to the underwear department.

But Julia seemed to know her mind, even about underwear. Within two minutes, she was ready to check out.

"That's it? Don't you want to shop longer?" he asked, looking at his watch. They'd only been in the store fifteen minutes. The last shopping trip he'd taken, for someone other than himself, had lasted hours.

They stepped outside, her purchases neatly folded in a plastic bag that he insisted on carrying, and the limo pulled up.

After they were settled inside, Julia said, "I'll have to admit one thing, James. You make a shopping trip easy."

The chauffeur said, "Thank you, ma'am."

"Hey, how about me? I carried your bag," Nick protested, not used to being ranked second, below the chauffeur.

"Yes, and it was such a strain, wasn't it?"

Nick ground his teeth. As president of the corporation that owned a dozen hotels, he was used to a lot more respect than Julia gave him. And that job had not just been handed to him. He'd worked in every department in the hotel business from the time he turned sixteen. Even when attending college, he'd worked part-time. When his father had retired, even he'd believed Nick was prepared to take over.

Whatever differences they had, there were none about his management of the business. No, their problems usually dealt with his father's search for love.

Nick knew his mother and father had had a wonderful marriage. But his father's second wife had ended all his thoughts of romantic love, if not his father's. She'd been after the money, like most women.

Even Julia's mother, in spite of what Julia thought.

"Are you hungry?" Nick asked as they ended their silent ride to the penthouse.

"Yes. Is there somewhere nearby to eat?"

"Yes. How would you like your steak cooked?"

"Steak? No, I meant something simple. You know, a sandwich shop or something."

"If we don't eat here in the hotel, my chef will

probably resign, Julia. Please help me preserve peace around here."

"But—"

"I can have it delivered up here so we can be comfortable."

"Really, that's not necessary."

"Dinner will include slices of a Death by Chocolate cake that you won't believe," he added with a smile.

"Do they charge extra for that?" she asked softly.

"Julia, you can't—" He broke off as he saw a distinct twinkle in her blue eyes. In relief, he smiled. "Yeah, they charge double for the cake. Deal?"

"Deal," she agreed. "By the way, I like my steak well done."

"The chef is going to complain," Nick warned.

"Just remind him that the customer is always right."

He called the kitchen and made the order while Julia went to the room she'd chosen for the night to clean up.

As he hung up the phone, he realized he was smiling. He hadn't looked forward to dinner in years. Could it be Julia?

That was a ridiculous thought. But he had to admit she was different from his usual dinner companions. But then, so had been their shopping excursion. And their flight. And their lunch at the Mansion. Weirdest of all had been their meeting at the Hotel Luna.

His smile widened. Yes, Julia was different.

Julia heard Nick call her to dinner, but she didn't go immediately to the living room. She was too busy warning herself to stop falling for her adversary. Just because he had occasional moments of charm didn't mean he'd accept her mother's marriage to his father. She knew that. And she could never be with Nick otherwise.

With a deep breath and a promise to be on her guard, Julia opened the door to her room.

Nick looked up and smiled at her, and she almost retreated behind a closed door again. Instead, she entered the living room, looking at the table set with silver and candles. A waiter was unloading dishes from a linen-covered cart and placing them on the table. He murmured something to Nick that Julia couldn't hear. Then he leaned over and lit the two candles. As a final act, he lowered the living room light.

Then he disappeared. Julia stepped closer, feeling the candlelight on her face. "My, did they leave any food for the other guests in the hotel?"

"A few scraps," Nick said. "I thought it was time you had a decent meal."

"I think you've exceeded decent, Nick. I didn't intend for you to go to such extremes."

"Just relax and enjoy. I think my father owes you at least this much."

"Well, maybe one of the Ramplings does," she said coolly.

"Wait a minute. Are you saying all of this is my fault?"

She sat down at the table, taking a sip of her iced tea before she answered. "It seems to me that your

father had anticipated your condemnation of his behavior. Were he not afraid of your actions, he
could've come to Houston with my mother and met
me. Then we could've planned a quiet wedding, not
this ridiculous chase."

"If that's the way you feel, why are you here with
me?" Nick asked.

"Because I want to protect my mother."

"Oh, yeah, I forgot," he said dryly.

He served her a salad without speaking. Then he
sat down to enjoy his own. After several minutes of
silence, he said, "If I promise to be nice to your
mother, will you go back to Houston?"

"No."

He wasn't sure why he'd even asked that question,
because Julia's disappearance would take away the
enjoyment he was having, which, of course, was totally wrong of him. His father hadn't eloped just to
entertain his son.

"You don't trust me?" Another stupid question.

"I trust you to do what *you* think is right, but I'm
not sure you'll understand my mother's feelings."

"I understand she'll be disappointed, but I told
you I always offer a decent reward for women taking their claws off my father's bank account."

"And that approach explains my concern. My
mother wouldn't know how to get into Abe's bank
account. I've no doubt she's married Abe because she
loves him. She'll be appalled that you would offer
to buy her off. That's why I need to be there."

Nick gave her a stern look. "You're assuming

they're married. My dad could just be having a pleasant interlude."

"Then why are we going to Vegas?"

"To try to find them. People go to Vegas for other reasons, you know." Nick grinned. "Maybe they went to gamble."

Julia didn't respond. Instead, she kept her head down, calmly eating her salad.

Nick prompted her. "You don't have anything to say about how your mother would never gamble? So far, you've acted as if she were a saint."

"She's not a saint, but she's not like the women your father apparently associates with."

Nick didn't respond to her challenge. He was pretty sure Lois Chance was quite a bit like her daughter. If that were true, he wasn't sure how easy it would be to sever his father's relationship with her.

Julia interrupted his thoughts. "Have you made the reservations for our flight to Las Vegas?"

"No, I haven't. I'll call the desk and have them make the reservations."

"Please ask for coach for my ticket."

"Julia, I'd rather—"

"My choice has nothing to do with you."

With a growl, he called the front desk and asked someone to make the reservations for them. When he said his companion wanted a ticket in coach, there was a shocked silence.

"Sir, you don't want to sit beside your companion?"

He knew the woman had asked that question to be sure of getting the right tickets, but he was embarrassed. He always bought the best for his companions. "That's right."

He chose the 9:00 a.m. flight, receiving an approving nod from Julia. Somehow he'd known that sleeping late wouldn't be in her plans.

When he hung up the phone, Julia asked, "Do we pay for our tickets when we get to the airport?"

"Yeah, at the counter." Then he rose and served their dinners.

Julia seemed to enjoy her steak, eating almost all of it.

He liked seeing a woman with a healthy appetite. At the Mansion, he'd feared Julia was one of those women who wouldn't eat in front of a man. He hated that kind of behavior.

"Do you have a hotel in Vegas?" Julia suddenly asked.

"No, but we exchange our suites with a hotel there that gives us the same privileges."

She frowned.

"What's wrong?"

"I suppose you frequently have…companions with you."

The censure that he saw in her eyes irritated him. He'd admit that he'd had more than his share of companions, though almost none in recent years. He'd been too busy with work. But he wasn't going to admit that to Julia. He leaned back and drawled, "It makes traveling more fun."

"And that's why you think your father may just be having a fling, rather than having eloped."

"Yeah."

"I see." She folded her napkin onto her plate and rose. "If you'll excuse me, I believe I shall retire early to be up in time for the flight in the morning."

"Not yet. You forgot the chocolate cake." He uncovered the dessert, two large slices of the Death by Chocolate cake.

"No, thank you." She walked away from the table.

Nick followed her, reaching her before she could get to the bedroom door. "Wait, Julia. You like chocolate. Come on back and eat your dessert."

"I don't feel like chocolate tonight."

"What did I say to upset you?"

She turned to him and said, "I don't know your father. It may be possible that he has tricked my mother into thinking he meant marriage when he had no such thing in mind. That thought makes me feel rather ill…and all the more anxious to find her. Good night."

She pulled her arm free from his grasp and opened her door, quickly shutting it in Nick's face.

"Damn," he muttered. He'd finally convinced her of what he hoped had happened, and it bothered him. He didn't want Julia upset by his father's behavior. Nor did he like the condemnation he'd seen in her eyes when she'd looked at him.

He muttered to himself about it being a free country, but he didn't even convince himself. The women who had accompanied him in the past had done so in order to get things for themselves. Julia wasn't like that.

Nick returned to the table with a weary sigh. It seemed as if with every turn, he upset Julia. That had not been his intent. He admired her determination to care for her mother. He supposed her protectiveness came from her job. She probably took care of the young children in her classroom as if they were her very own.

That thought led him to wonder why she didn't have children of her own…and a doting husband. He didn't really like that thought, at least the husband part of it.

And he didn't want to ask why.

He picked up a fork and took a bite of the cake. He'd have to eat some of each piece to convince the chef that they appreciated his special dessert. He'd prefer to leave it uneaten and tell the waiter they'd been busy with another activity. If he added a wink, the waiter would tell the chef that Mr. Rampling was making love to his guest…but Julia wouldn't like that.

Not that people wouldn't think he was making love to Julia anyway. That was the reason for a companion, wasn't it? Which she had also condemned.

The cake was rich and he had to force himself to eat at least half of each piece. When he'd done that, he called for the waiter to return to collect the dirty dishes.

Once that had happened, Nick debated watching some television, but he finally went to bed, hoping tomorrow would turn out to be a better day.

Julia woke up early since she'd gone to bed at nine o'clock. After taking a shower and dressing in her new clothes, she packed her bag before she opened her bedroom door. There was no sign of Nick. His bedroom door was closed and she assumed he was still sleeping.

She decided to take her suitcase and go downstairs and have breakfast in the coffee shop. That would be the best way to show the staff that she was not Nick's companion.

When she arrived downstairs, she asked the bell-hop to take care of her bag while she had breakfast. That act alone caused a lot of whispering among the front desk personnel. One of them hurried to her side. "Ma'am, may I help you with anything?"

"No, thank you. I'm just going in the coffee shop to have breakfast."

Though the young lady looked at Julia strangely, she was pleasant and insisted on accompanying Julia to the door of the coffee shop. When she had the hostess seat Julia in Mr. Rampling's booth, Julia protested.

"No, that's not necessary," she assured the hostess.

"But, ma'am, that's the only booth open. If you don't eat there, you won't get seated for half an hour."

"Very well, but please treat me like any other customer."

"Of course, ma'am."

Since a waiter appeared instantly at her table, Julia was sure the hostess had not taken her seriously. Nevertheless she ordered her stack of pancakes and a glass of milk. After all, she wasn't a martyr.

Her meal was half-eaten when she heard a stir in the lobby. She continued to eat, hoping it had nothing to do with her. However, Nick was escorted to the coffee shop by the young lady who had done the same for her, and guided by the hostess into the large booth Julia occupied by herself.

Julia wanted to tell him she wasn't inclined to share, but that didn't seem fair since it was his booth. She looked up, however, and was shocked when he leaned over and kissed her.

She jerked her head away, prepared to rake him over the coals for his behavior, but he put his arm around her and smiled.

"Good morning, Julia, my dear. I didn't realize you'd be such an early riser. I can't believe I slept right through you getting up and taking your shower."

She was about to explain that the doors had been closed, but he leaned forward and said, "Don't make me kiss you again."

She caught the implication at once. Leaning closer to him, she whispered, "Don't make me dump the rest of my breakfast in your lap!"

"No, thanks, honey, I'll order my own. See, here's our waiter now. I'll have the same as Julia, please, only I'd like a cup of coffee. Don't you want some coffee, Julia?"

"Yes, I'll have a cup of coffee now, please," she said, smiling at the waiter.

Then she continued eating, ignoring the man next to her in the circular booth.

"I don't think you can convince them you don't know me, honey, so why don't you give up trying and speak to me."

Keeping her voice pleasant, she said, "Why should I want to talk to you when you've done your best to ruin my good name?"

"Come on, Julia, even second-grade teachers aren't expected to be celibate these days."

"So if you were putting your second grader in my class, you wouldn't mind if I slept with whomever came along? You'd feel comfortable with her having a slut as her teacher?"

Chapter Five

"You're being ridiculous," Nick said. "They won't even know."

"Word gets around this hotel fast enough. Got a hotel in Houston?" she asked in a hard voice.

"Yes, we do," he said with a frown. It hadn't occurred to him that it would matter. "I'm sure Houston won't hear about anything happening here."

"I wish I could be as certain," Julia said. "But I can't be, so make sure you don't kiss me again, whatever the reason."

"No one would expect you to go kissless, Julia."

"Of course not, but since we spent the night together, what would they expect when you kiss me in public?"

Nick didn't like the way the conversation was

going. He'd actually enjoyed the kiss he'd shared with Julia, even though he'd intended it as teasing punishment for walking out on him this morning. Fortunately, it had only taken a phone call to find out where she was, but he didn't like admitting that he'd lost track of her.

"You'd better eat your breakfast. We don't want to miss our flight." He hoped his words would distract her. His breakfast arrived, with an extra cup of coffee for Julia.

He spent the next few minutes eating, glad for the excuse not to carry on a conversation. He had just put the last bite in his mouth when Julia suggested they leave at once for the airport.

"Can't I at least have a few sips of coffee?" he asked.

She stared at him without answering.

He took two sips and set his mug down. "Okay, I'm ready." He offered a smile that she ignored.

They exited opposite ends of the booth and almost bumped into each other.

"Wait!" Julia exclaimed. "We haven't paid the bill."

"Honey, we don't pay for meals here. I own it, remember?"

She started to protest but stopped. Instead, she took out a ten-dollar bill and left it on the table.

"I told you you didn't have to pay," Nick said.

"I didn't. I left a tip," she assured him and sailed past him.

He took a deep breath, then shrugged his shoulders and followed her out of the coffee shop. Apparently she had signaled the bellhop to bring their bags. Nick stepped forward and told him to put the bags in the limo.

Nick held the door open for Julia to leave the hotel. James was waiting, holding the door to the limo open.

"Good to see you again, James," Julia said with a smile.

Nick nodded at his employee, determined not to be jealous of the smile James had received. Why couldn't Julia smile at *him* like that?

After a silent ride to the airport, James handed a skycap their bags and bid them a good day. "Have a nice flight," he said with a nod.

"Thank you, James." Julia blessed him with another bright smile.

Nick paused to give his chauffeur a tip, as he usually did, but suddenly he was self-conscious about it. "Thanks, James."

They both purchased their tickets to Las Vegas. Nick told himself not to feel bad about Julia flying coach. It was her choice. She knew he'd buy her a first-class ticket if she wanted one. They moved to the waiting area and sat down.

Nick frowned when he noticed Julia drawing looks from some of the men in the area. He took another look at her. Slender, with long blond hair and big blue eyes, she was beautiful, of course, but not a knockout, like some of the models and starlets he'd traveled with.

She looked up at that instant and he suddenly knew what it was about Julia that drew other men's gazes. It was her wholesomeness. She didn't look bored, jaded or pouty. She looked sweet and kind and...loving. Julia Chance was the kind of woman every man knew his mother would be glad to see walking through the door on his arm.

Just then, the boarding of their flight was announced, beginning with first class.

Nick didn't move. He preferred to sit there and look at her for a while longer.

Dangerous...

He ignored the warning voice inside his head.

Julia turned to look at him, her eyebrows raised in question. "Aren't you going to board?"

Feeling as if he had been caught doing something illegal, he assumed a nonchalant tone. "There's no rush."

The gate attendant quickly moved on to board the rest of the plane. Julia patiently waited until her row was called. When it was, she stood and picked up her suitcase.

"I'll get it," Nick said, putting his hand over hers.

"Nonsense," Julia insisted. "You have your own bag to take care of. I'll be fine." She tugged her bag from his grip and walked off.

"Damn it, Julia, I want to be sure you board without any problems. Quit running away!" He caught up with her in time to walk down the jetway to the plane.

"I'm perfectly capable of boarding a plane by

myself. After all, I've flown more than a few times in my twenty-six years."

Nick sighed. She was right, of course, but he still hadn't liked leaving her alone in the waiting room. Or leaving her at all, he admitted.

His seat in first class was in the last row, and Julia's seat in coach was in the tenth row. Not too far apart. As the plane prepared for departure he could even hear her light, musical tones—mixed with deeper masculine voices. Definitely more than one. Hell, it sounded as if she were entertaining a whole slew of men.

He started to undo his seat belt to go to see if she needed his protection, but the plane began to taxi and he knew he'd be told to sit down.

The seat beside Nick was empty. If he used his mileage points, he could get Julia moved up beside him. That would be a good idea. She wouldn't protest because he wasn't paying money for the seat. Why hadn't he thought of that before?

Because Julia confused him, distracted him, made him forget his own name.

As the plane leveled out at cruising altitude, the first-class flight attendant began taking drink orders and serving hot cinnamon buns.

What about in coach, he thought. Would they get only a drink and a tiny bag of pretzels? He almost growled out loud. He'd never worried about coach! Not until he'd met Miss Julia Chance.

When the flight attendant came to serve him, he said, "Miss, I have a friend in coach, and I'd like to use my mileage points to move her up here beside me."

"I'm sorry, sir, but those kind of arrangements have to be made before boarding." She handed him his coffee.

Nick turned on the charm, flashing her a white smile that made laugh lines around his eyes that his previous women had told him were oh so sexy. "I'm sorry, but I didn't think of it till now. Couldn't you make an exception?"

The brunette attendant leaned in a bit closer when she served his cinnamon bun and whispered conspiratorially, "Let me see what I can do."

A few minutes later, she came back. "Mission accomplished, Mr. Rampling." After he gave her Julia's name she said, "I'll go inform Miss Chance that it's her lucky day."

Nick sat back in his leather seat and sipped his coffee, pleased with himself. He looked forward to the rest of the flight with Julia at his side.

Instead of Julia, the brunette appeared beside him. "I'm sorry, Mr. Rampling, but Miss Chance declines your offer."

Without a word, Nick got up and moved down the aisle into coach. He found Julia sitting in the middle seat of row ten, talking and laughing with the two men who surrounded her.

Nick squared his jaw and stared at Julia until she looked up.

"Hi, Nick," she said, as if she didn't know why he was there.

"Julia, why didn't you join me?"

"Because I'm happy where I am, thank you."

"I went to a lot of trouble to arrange it," he told her, unfortunately letting his exasperation show.

"But I told you I pay my own way, Nick. I didn't ask you to move me up to first class. Thank you, anyway." She kept her voice pleasant, but he could see the stubborness as she raised her chin.

With a casual "Suit yourself," he strolled back to his seat as if he didn't have a care in the world. Inside, he was boiling.

He'd just made a fool of himself over a woman who didn't even want his money.

Julia knew she'd upset Nick; that hadn't been her intention, but she had to keep her distance from the man.

Time spent with her neighbors in row ten would certainly give her a break from Nick. And from his autocratic behavior.

When the plane landed in Las Vegas, Julia followed her fellow passengers down the aisle to the exit, wondering if it had been smart on her part to say no to Nick. What if he left without her? She wouldn't know where to look for her mother.

A sense of relief filled her when she saw Nick leaning against the wall, a bored look on his face.

"Thanks for waiting for me, Nick," she said, looking at him hopefully.

"I'm not sure I should've, after your behavior on the plane."

"I told you I would pay my own way. Didn't you believe me?"

"Damn it, I was using my mileage points, Julia, not money."

"Let's just forget it. What do we do now?"

"We—" Nick was interrupted by his phone ringing. He pulled it out of his jacket and answered. "Oh. Thanks, Pat."

"What did he say?" Julia asked.

"He's arranged a limo to pick us up."

"All right."

"No, you don't understand. He's arranged the *same* limo that Dad used."

"Which one?" Julia asked as they moved out of the terminal.

"He should be holding a sign with my name on it," Nick said. He scanned the group of limo drivers, some holding signs with passengers' names on them, others offering their services to anyone who came along.

"There he is," Julia said in a low voice.

Nick followed Julia's gaze and saw a short, stubby man holding a sign as high as he could with Nick's name on it.

"All right, let's go," he said, taking Julia's arm. He was relieved that she was back beside him. Just because he felt protective, of course. It had nothing to do with Julia. It was merely his sense of responsibility.

Even he wouldn't buy that.

"I'm Rampling," he said to the driver.

"Yes, sir, Mr. Rampling. Your man, Mr. Browning, said you wanted to hire me."

Nick wondered how his father had hired this man. "Yes. We want you to take us to the same place you took my father three days ago."

The driver smacked his forehead in a comic manner. "O' course! That's why your name sounded familiar! Like father, like son, eh? Well, you got yourself a beauty, just like your old man."

"Will you do as we asked?" Nick said, ignoring the man's boisterous welcome.

"O' course I will! Right this way. Step into my limousine of love!" He drew out the last word, like a bad lounge singer.

Nick cringed, finding it difficult to submit to this man's uncouth behavior. He indicated Julia should precede him. As he ducked to follow her into the vehicle, he heard a soft giggle. Surprised, he looked at her questioningly.

Julia covered her mouth, but her eyes were dancing.

"What?" he whispered.

"This man is just too much. I think my mother would've been overwhelmed by his—shtick," she whispered.

He'd put his arm around her as she'd leaned toward him to whisper and he left it there. It felt good.

The moment the driver started his vehicle, the music of Elvis Presley poured into the air. It started with "Viva Las Vegas." Before Nick could get over his astonishment and request silence, the music changed to "Love Me Tender."

He looked at Julia and discovered her silently giggling. A reluctant smile crossed his face. She was enjoying the schmaltzy turnout. Had his father and Julia's mother enjoyed it, too?

Suddenly he remembered he hadn't seen his father laugh in a long time. Strange thought.

"Are you sure he remembers where he took our parents?" Julia whispered.

"I hope so. And I hope it's soon."

She giggled again, softly, and he pulled her a little closer, unable to resist.

Later, when the limo pulled to a halt, the little man came around to open Nick's door. "Here we are, my lovebirds! The newest Chapel Amore!"

"This is where you brought my father and his lady friend?" Nick asked to be sure.

"Yes, sir!" he said in his booming voice. "And the blushing bride loved it!"

Nick thought he couldn't have been more obnoxious if he'd used a bullhorn.

Julia gave the man a bright smile and whispered to Nick, "At least he didn't announce us by name."

"Good point," Nick agreed. He stepped forward and pulled out his billfold to give the man a hundred-dollar bill. "As promised," he said.

Almost in the blink of an eye, the man had pocketed the money and driven away.

"But don't we need him to take us wherever we need to go afterward?" Julia asked.

"No, we can get a taxi without the Elvis music," he told her.

"That was pretty awful, wasn't it?" Julia giggled again.

"Yeah." Picking up both their bags, he nodded with his head for Julia to precede him into the Chapel Amore.

Julia found it hard to imagine that her mother had gotten married here. Her parents' wedding had been in a small church back in their hometown of Whitney, Texas, thirty-four years ago.

A very traditional wedding.

Not what happened in the Chapel Amore.

A sweet, white-haired woman greeted them as they entered.

"Welcome, my dears. You've chosen a wonderful day for your wedding. Here, put your bags right down. They'll be safe until after the wedding."

Then before they could explain why they were there, she turned and walked through a side door.

"Where did she go?" Julia asked.

Nick shrugged his shoulders.

Again, the woman appeared suddenly, carrying a bouquet of plastic flowers, which she thrust into Julia's hands, and a veil. She reached up to place it on Julia's head.

Automatically, Julia ducked, but the woman managed to get the veil on her anyway.

"Now, have you ever seen a prettier bride?" the woman cooed.

"No," Nick said, "but we're not here to get married."

The woman stared at him. "Then why would you come to the Chapel Amore?"

"We want to know if you married an Abe Rampling and a Lois Chance three days ago."

The sweetness disappeared from her face and Julia thought she looked greedy and mean. "We're not an information center. We only perform marriages."

"How much does it take to have a wedding?" Nick asked, not wasting time.

"Seventy-five dollars."

"Okay." He reached into his wallet and held up a bill. "Here's a hundred bucks. Now, I want the information. If I get it, you get the money," he said, holding the bill just out of the woman's quick reach.

"How do I know you won't leave after I give you the information?"

"You don't." Nick paused and then handed the money to Julia. "She'll give you the money if she's satisfied. You can trust her more than me." Before Julia could protest, he asked the woman, "Well, do we have a deal?"

"Yeah. Billy, bring out the register!" the woman yelled.

Another door opened and a man in a black coat with a white collar entered, a smile on his face. When he saw his wife's expression, he asked, "What's going on here?"

"They want to see the register. They want to know about that nice couple we married a few days ago. Mr. and Mrs. Rampling."

"Why?" the man growled.

"Because we're paying a hundred dollars for the information," Nick growled in return.

As if he'd said a magic word, the man opened the register for Nick and showed him where he'd recorded the marriage of one Abe Rampling, 56, and one Lois Chance, 52, four days ago.

"*Four* days ago? They left Los Angeles the same day they arrived and came here?" Julia asked.

"Apparently so," Nick said softly. "We're four days behind instead of three."

"So we gave you the information, right?" the woman asked Julia.

"Yes, you did." Julia handed her the money. "Thank you."

"We need a taxi," Nick said. "Can you please call one for us?"

"We ain't no taxi stand, neither." The woman put her hands on her hips. The hundred-dollar bill wasn't in sight.

Julia stared at the woman. "After a nice tip like you just got, you don't have the decency to call us a cab?"

"Fine! I'll call you a cab. But it'll take a few minutes to get here. Do you want to sit in the waiting room? 'Cause that'll cost you!"

"No, thank you," Julia said before Nick could answer. She wasn't going to let him waste another penny on these two. "After you call for the taxi, we'll wait outside."

She stood there with her arms crossed over her

chest as the woman made the call. Then she turned and walked out of the Chapel Amore.

Nick followed her. "I hope you don't regret not staying in the waiting room," he said as they stood in the incredible heat of summer in the desert.

"How can you even think of offering that greedy woman any more money! She—she— I'll swelter in the sun for an hour before I pay her more money!"

Nick gave her a little hug. "Good for you."

"Oh, Nick, I hate to think Mom got married with those people instead of having her family around her!"

Nick gave her a droll look. "I hate it, too."

"Yes, but you hate it because you don't want them married at all."

"True," Nick said with a sigh.

"What are you going to do?"

"Find them."

"I meant immediately."

"I suggest we get out of this town, unless you want to do some gambling."

Julia gave him an appalled look. "No!" she exclaimed. "But what if they are staying here?"

"I don't think so. They're making too big an effort to be way ahead of us. In fact, I think I know where they are. So we go to the airport. Without the Elvis serenade this time."

"Where do you think they are?"

"Either in San Francisco or Hawaii."

"Why those two places?" Julia asked.

"Because my father would plan a perfect honeymoon, I'm sure. And for him, those are the two best places on Earth."

Julia looked around at the tacky surroundings. "I have to admit, Las Vegas wouldn't be my mother's choice for a honeymoon, I'm sure."

"Yours either, I'd guess," Nick said on a laugh.

She shared his grin. "Right on that count."

They waited only a few more minutes before the taxi arrived.

The driver got out to take their luggage and put it in the trunk as they got into the back seat. He received their request for the airport with a smile and started his taxi in that direction.

And Elvis began singing "Viva Las Vegas"!

Chapter Six

Once they were settled side by side on the plane—in coach, since all the first-class seats were sold out—Julia asked, "So what do we do now?"

"As soon as we get back to L.A., I'll call Pat. He'll check out the airlines for us."

"How long will it take?"

"Not long."

Julia couldn't hold back a smile. "You should've called him before we left, but I bet you were in a hurry because you wanted to get away from hearing Elvis sing 'Viva Las Vegas.'"

Nick grinned. "You've got a point there. I do believe that song scrambled my brain."

"How do you think they got out of the hotel so quickly without anyone seeing them?"

Nick closed his eyes for a minute. Then he opened them. "They could've gone down in the freight elevator and slipped out a side door. Dad knows the hotel like an old friend. If they walked a block to the next hotel, they could've found a taxi. And because they told them they wouldn't need service and put a Do Not Disturb sign on the door, no one thought anything about it."

"They're being very clever, aren't they?"

"Yes. And I know you're going to say it's my fault."

Julia grimaced. "Well, I think it is, because Mom would never think of hiding anything."

"Are you sure of that? Never?"

Julia quickly thought about her mother's life. "I'm sure she has some secrets, but not a marriage. She certainly couldn't expect to hide something like that from me."

"My father doesn't expect to hide his marriage from me, either. He just expects to hide it long enough that I can't manage to arrange an annulment."

"Is that what you intend to do?" she said slowly, staring at him. "Why would you do that if they've fallen in love? Do you hate the idea of your father having someone to share his life with?"

Nick chose his answer carefully. She made it sound as if he were a monster even to contemplate an annulment for his father. "I know it sounds harsh, Julia, but my father doesn't have a stellar record with women."

"So you automatically assume any woman he chooses is bad?"

"I've been proved right every time so far." He hated the disappointment on her face. "You don't know how he's been, Julia. He says he gets so lonely, but the only women I've found attached to his pocketbook are twenty-five-year-olds who think they've found a sugar daddy. I'm saving Dad's pride by buying them off." He tried to steel himself against her emotional appeal. Suddenly he realized if her mother was anything like Julia, he was in trouble. But he couldn't allow himself to think like that.

When she spoke, her voice was two octaves higher, and a lot louder. "We're talking about my mother! And I won't allow you to say those horrible things about her. She's not like the other women!"

"Calm down. If your mother is truly in love with my father—not his money—maybe I'll back off. She can sign a prenuptial agreement and it will all be settled."

"How can it be a *pre*nuptial agreement? They're already married."

"Whatever. If she's willing to forgo any claim to our money, then she can have Dad."

She gave him a strange stare. "You really don't believe in love, do you, Nick?"

"And you do?"

"Yes, I do. My parents were married for thirty-two years. They shared everything, the good and the bad, and they still loved each other very much. Mom was devastated by Dad's death two years ago."

"They were the exception to the rule, you know, not the norm."

Julia stared at him. "You've never loved anyone?"

"You may not believe it, but I love my dad." He just had to work extra hard to protect his father from himself.

"No, I mean—have you ever been *in* love?" She cocked her head to the side as she stared at him, waiting for an answer.

He leaned toward her and lowered his voice. "I've been in lust, Julia, more than once. When I was young, I thought it was love. But time proved me wrong."

"I—I feel sorry for you, Nick."

Her unwanted sympathy irritated him. "I don't need you to feel sorry for me, Julia. I'm just fine the way I am. And if you think love is so important, why aren't you married?" He was very interested in her answer. Ever since he saw her standing there in a bridal veil, holding a bouquet, he'd felt unsettled.

"You can't just decide to fall in love." She shrugged her shoulders. "I hope to fall in love one day. It just hasn't happened for me yet."

He saw the longing in her eyes, in her voice, and he felt a response in himself that scared the hell out of him. He wasn't a "falling in love" kind of guy. He didn't think his father was, either. Abe always said he'd loved Nick's mother, but she'd died shortly after Nick was born and within a few years Abe had remarried.

Thankfully, the woman had left after three years of misery. And she'd taken a chunk of money with her. Other women had come and gone, but his father had never married any of them. Until now.

"So, what if it never happens to you? Do you spend your life waiting for 'love'?" Nick asked, letting his scorn for the word be heard in his voice.

Julia turned away from him. "Never mind."

Nick fought the urge to touch her, to offer comfort, to assure her that her dream would come true. But he couldn't do that, because he didn't believe it…did he?

That was the scariest thing about Julia. She made him want to believe in love, in happily-ever-after, and he was afraid of that kind of change.

He straightened his shoulders. He was a tough businessman. Julia's soft thoughts were not appropriate in his life. He had to remain strong.

Leaning forward, he took the in-flight magazine out of the pocket of the seat in front of him and nonchalantly pretended to read it, as if he didn't care that he'd hurt the woman next to him.

Julia wasn't sure what had happened. For a little while, she and Nick had seemed in sync, as if their thoughts were flowing in the same direction. Then, he had changed, rejecting the possibility that their parents had happily wed in Las Vegas.

Julia could only hope he was wrong. She suddenly realized what she'd thought. There was no doubt that he was wrong. Her mother would never marry for money. If she and Abe were married, then Lois intended it to be for all time. And it was Julia's job to help make that true.

Was Abe like his son? And if so, why had he married Lois? Julia closed her eyes, offering a silent prayer for her mother's happiness.

She turned back around to see Nick reading a magazine. She couldn't believe he could be so cold about his father's happiness. "Where do we go when we get back to L.A.?" she asked abruptly.

"Back to the hotel until we find out where they've gone," Nick said without looking up.

"I think I should get a room. It won't look good for us to share the suite again."

His eyes still on the magazine, he said, "That's fine with me, but unless you have unlimited funds, you might want to save your money for wherever they've gone. Then again, you could leave it to me to find them."

"No!" She paused, thinking about what he had said. "Do you really think they've gone to San Francisco or Hawaii?"

"Knowing my dad, I think it's likely. But he may have decided to visit Hong Kong."

"That far?" Julia responded with a gasp. She had a nice savings account, but she'd already made serious inroads into it. Finally, she conceded, "All right, if you don't mind, I'll stay in the suite with you."

"Sure, why not?"

"But I don't want you kissing me in public. It gives people the wrong idea. Promise?"

"Sure, no problem."

His casual dismissal of the kiss eased her worry. Obviously, it hadn't meant anything to him. She could pretend the same, couldn't she? She had to. If she wasn't careful, this man—this difficult, pragmatic, unbelieving man—could break her heart.

When the plane landed, Julia hurried off the plane ahead of Nick. Why, she didn't know. It wasn't as if she could get away from him. Not if she wanted to protect her mother's happiness. After she entered the airport, she turned to wait for Nick.

He wasn't too far behind her.

"Do you think James will have the limo here for us?"

"No. I didn't let him know. We can just take a taxi," Nick said, taking her arm, as if he were afraid she'd get away.

When they reached the sidewalk, they were both surprised to discover James waiting by the limo.

"James, who told you we'd be back this soon?" Nick asked.

"No one, sir. I'm supposed to pick up a couple arriving on their honeymoon from Seattle. But there'll be plenty of room for the two of you."

Nick frowned. "Let's wait for our guests and see if they'll mind."

"Yes, sir." James stood there for a moment before he asked, "Was your trip to Las Vegas enjoyable?"

"We're not sure just yet, James, but thank you for asking." Nick turned to Julia. "Do you mind waiting? We can go ahead and take a taxi."

"I don't mind waiting, if you think the other couple won't mind."

"Hello? Are you the limo from the Rampling Hotel?" a young man asked.

James stepped forward and reached for the two large suitcases he carried. "Yes, sir. And may I present the owner of the hotel?" He nodded toward Nick. "Would you mind if he and his guest shared your ride to the hotel?"

"Of course not. Uh, honey, you don't mind, do you?"

A shy young woman stepped forward. "No, of course not. I've never ridden in a limousine before, but they're supposed to be big, aren't they?"

Nick smiled at her. "I can assure you there's ample room for four of us. Maybe for eight of us."

"Oh, are there others who need a ride?" the young lady asked, looking around her.

"No, I was just joking. I'm glad to welcome you to the hotel. I hope you'll enjoy your visit."

"We will," the man said. "It's our honeymoon."

"Good for you," Nick said. "I'll make sure our concierge shows you some special events for newlyweds. I think you'll enjoy them."

"Well, thanks," the gentleman said. "Where did you two fly in from?"

"Las Vegas," Nick replied.

"Oh, no," he said with a grin. "Don't tell me you went to one of those crazy marriage places?"

"I'm afraid so," Nick admitted.

With so much on her mind, Julia hadn't paid much attention to the conversation. But something about what had just been said seemed to sound a warning in her head. Before she could say anything or ask any questions, the limo arrived at the hotel.

Nick shook the man's hand and thanked them for sharing the limo. Then he picked up their two bags and indicated she should precede him into the hotel.

Instead of heading directly for the elevators, he stopped by the registration desk. "The couple following us in is on their honeymoon. Make sure the concierge offers them the honeymoon package at my expense."

"Yes, sir, Mr. Rampling," the clerk said, a surprised look on his face.

Then Nick led Julia to the elevator. "Glad to be back in my hotel?" he asked with a teasing look as they entered the elevator.

"It certainly seems to make you happier," Julia said. He'd been withdrawn and had scarcely talked since their discussion on the plane, which hadn't ended well.

"Well, it beats what we saw in Vegas."

"Speaking of Vegas, what was it you said about Las Vegas in the limo?"

"Weren't you listening?"

"No, I wasn't."

"The man asked if we'd visited one of those crazy marriage places," Nick said as the elevator door opened onto the penthouse suite.

"And you said yes?"

"Of course I did. It's true, isn't it?"

"Yes, but you did explain why, didn't you?"

"It was none of their business, Julia."

She followed him into the suite. "But, Nick, it's possible he thought we went there to get married!"

"Don't be silly. There's no reason he'd think that."

* * *

"Welcome, Mr. and Mrs. Nelson. We hope your stay with us will be a happy one," the man at the reception desk said as the couple came into the hotel.

"Thank you. I'm sure we will enjoy ourselves," Mr. Nelson said.

"Our owner, Mr. Rampling, asked me to offer you the honeymoon events package at his expense as a thank-you for sharing the limo with them."

"He did? Wow! That's really nice that someone on his own honeymoon would take the time to think about us."

"On his own honeymoon? I think you must be—"

"Mistaken? No, I asked him. He said they'd been to Vegas to visit one of those marriage places. He and his wife seemed quite happy."

"I see. Well, enjoy yourselves and if there's anything we can do to make your stay more enjoyable, please let us know."

The registration clerk remained in place until the couple entered the elevator. Then he grabbed his supervisor and told him what the man had said.

"Mr. Rampling got married in Vegas? Oh, no, we must prepare a celebration! You go tell the chef to make a wedding cake." He turned to the other clerk and then the assistant concierge. "Miss Wilson, arrange for a wedding bouquet for the suite at once. Karl, you must go to Neiman's and find a suitable wedding present from the staff. Have it gift wrapped there. What else shall we need?"

"Do we want wedding decorations for the suite?" someone ventured.

The supervisor thought for a moment. "No, I think not. Mr. Rampling is understated." After another moment of thought, he said, "No, I think a simple celebration with the staff will be all that will be required. Oh, and be sure we have several bottles of our best champagne on ice."

There was a new wave of excitement among the staff at the celebration in the works.

"I think I'll go to the coffee shop and get a sandwich," Julia said stiffly after she'd settled back into the same bedroom she'd used before.

Nick had been pouring himself a glass of bottled water at the bar. He looked up. "I'll go with you."

"Have you already talked to Pat?"

"Yeah, I called him after you went in your room. He said he'd try to get back to us tonight, but it might be tomorrow morning before he can."

"But maybe tonight?"

"I wouldn't hold my breath, Julia. There are a lot of flights to check."

"Yes, I know."

"Cheer up, Julia. You're not exactly going to suffer while you're waiting." He was a little irritated by her attitude. She had the services of a five-star hotel and she was disappointed?

"No, of course not."

He put down the glass and followed her out of the

suite. "Of course, we could've had lunch sent up to us," he reminded her.

"I don't see the point in making the staff work harder when we're capable of going down."

Nick rolled his eyes, but he didn't say anything.

When they reached the lobby, they started toward the coffee shop. Immediately, one of the men from behind the desk hurried toward them.

"Mr. Rampling, how may we help you, sir?"

"We don't need anything, Sid. We're just going in the coffee shop for an early lunch."

"Don't you want us to serve you in the suite?"

"Julia wants to eat with everyone else, and I'm trying to accommodate her. We'll order dinner in the suite. How about that?"

"Oh, of course, sir. We must keep the ladies happy, mustn't we?" he said with a soft laugh and a wink.

"Right." Nick returned the grin, though he wondered what was wrong with one of his best employees.

"Is anything wrong?" Julia asked softly.

"No, not really."

They walked to the door of the coffee shop and the hostess gasped.

"Oh! Right this way, Mr. Rampling," she said, leading them to his special booth, before she hurried back to take care of waiting guests.

"I think we've caused more of a disturbance by coming down here than if we had ordered upstairs," Nick muttered as they slid into the booth. "It must be you who's drawing all the attention. They don't act this way when it's just me."

Julia didn't respond. She studied the menu because she suspected the waiter would be at their table at once. She didn't want to prolong their lunch.

She wasn't wrong. The waiter stepped up and delivered two glasses of water and asked their drink preferences.

"I'll have iced tea," Julia said quietly.

"Bring me a cup of coffee, Jim, heavy on the caffeine."

The waiter smiled in sympathy. "Right, Mr. Rampling."

"You make it sound as if I've caused you to miss a lot of sleep," Julia pointed out, frowning.

"And that surprises you?" Nick asked, a grin on his face. She apparently had no idea how thoughts of her were disrupting his sleep.

"I think it's our parents who are causing both of us to miss sleep."

"Oh, yeah, that's what I meant," he said, his grin widening.

Chapter Seven

When the waiter arrived with their drinks, they ordered lunch.

"You know, you chose my favorite," Nick said, moving over to get more comfortable in the booth.

Julia sidled over a bit in the opposite direction. "Turkey club on whole wheat? I had no way of knowing." She put her head down and became quiet again.

Nick noticed her frown and tried to reassure her. "Don't worry, Julia. Pat will call as soon as he knows for sure. He doesn't do a halfway job."

Julia sighed. "I'm sorry to be so disagreeable. But I'm worried about Mom, and knowing what you have planned for them when you find them doesn't make me worry any less."

"I'd like to promise happily-ever-after to you, Julia, but I can't. At least, not until I've met your mother."

"But when you meet her you might give them your blessing?" Julia asked eagerly.

Nick leaned toward her. "Honey, it might happen, but the odds aren't in her favor. She'll refuse to sign the prenup, and that will open my father's eyes. Then it will all be over."

Tears filled Julia's eyes and she moved toward the edge of the booth, intending, Nick was sure, to leave him sitting there. Fortunately, Jim arrived with their lunch, and Julia settled back down.

"I'm glad you didn't leave," Nick said after Jim had gone away. "You would've made him think he'd done something wrong."

"I think you're glad because Jim would've understood that *you* are the one who did something wrong!"

"He wouldn't think that, sweetheart. After all, I'm his boss."

"Nick Rampling, you are spoiled rotten!"

He guessed there was some truth in that. No, actually he knew there was. He'd never really thought much about it. Until Julia. Unlike the other women in his life, she had the nerve to point it out to him.

He figured she deserved an honest reply. "Yeah, I guess so, but I didn't mean to upset you. I could've lied to you and said, yeah, there was a good chance I'd give them my blessings. But that's not the truth. I assumed you'd want the truth."

She was silent for a moment, then said, "Yes, I do. I'll try not to get emotional anymore."

Nick figured she could turn off the tears as easily as he could submerge his doubts. But he decided they were at a stalemate. At least he wasn't losing. Yet.

"Feel better?" he asked Julia after they had finished their lunch.

"The food certainly helped."

"Got any place you'd like to go this afternoon?"

Much to his surprise, her answer was, "Yes. I'd like to go to a bookstore."

He stepped over to the concierge's desk. "Where's the closest bookstore?"

"There's a Barnes & Noble four blocks away, Mr. Rampling. Shall I call James?"

Julia replied instead, "No, thank you. I'll walk."

Nick looked at her, then turned back to the concierge. "Never mind, Peter. *We'll* walk."

After they moved away from the desk, Julia whispered fiercely, "I don't need you to accompany me!"

"Maybe *I* want to go to the bookstore, too."

"Why?"

"I do read, Julia. If we're stuck on some more long flights, a book would help pass the time."

"I could bring you back a book."

"Selecting a book is a very personal thing. Even if you knew exactly what I like, how would you know if I'd already read it or not?" He put his hand on her back to guide her toward the closest door. "This way."

It was warm in Los Angeles this afternoon, and

the sun felt good as they walked in a leisurely fashion. "I'm glad you suggested this walk, Julia. It feels good to be outside."

"Yes, it does. And a little exercise will help you sleep better, too."

He smiled at her. "Yeah, I do usually get some exercise during the week. Dad kind of screwed up my schedule this week."

"What do you do for exercise?"

"I play racquetball."

"Ah. That's good exercise."

"You play?"

"I have, occasionally, but not normally. I do aerobics three or four times a week."

"No wonder you have such a good shape."

"What did you say?" she asked, glaring at him.

"Um, I said, no wonder you're *in* such good shape. You're not even breathing heavily." He added a smile.

"We haven't been exactly racing, Nick," Julia pointed out.

"No, but we've been moving at a good pace. Though I don't know why. We're not in a hurry." He intentionally slowed down.

She gave him a sharp look, but she slowed down, too. "I guess we might as well enjoy our stroll."

And they did. Or at least Nick suspected she did. They talked about books—what they'd read, what they liked—and discovered they shared a penchant for mysteries.

Before he knew it, they'd arrived at the bookstore. "Here we are."

"Oh, I didn't realize we were so close," Julia said as she entered the door he held open.

"Where do you want to start looking?"

She looked up at him. "You're not one of those people who rushes through a bookstore, are you?"

"No. Take your time. Come find me when you're ready," he said, and wandered to the magazine section. He didn't want to crowd her in the mystery aisle.

Half an hour later, he'd found two books he wanted, and settled down in a comfortable chair to start reading. He felt sure Julia could find him when she was ready.

He was several chapters into one of his choices before she appeared, holding several books in her arms. "Are you ready?" she asked, a little breathless.

"Sure, but there's no hurry. Do you have everything you want?"

"Yes, I think so," she said, clutching her books to her.

"Did you buy any mysteries?"

"A couple. I'll show you mine if you show me yours."

She said it so deadpan, Nick suspected she hadn't meant the double entendre. Then she let loose with a smile.

"I'm game," he said, playing along. He handed her his books, and she reciprocated.

"I might be willing to make a trade after I've read mine," she said, handing his books back.

"You're on. I'm willing to share." He smiled at her, pleased with their afternoon. He'd never spent time talking about books with a woman. And she didn't even want him to pay for them.

On the walk back to the hotel, they passed an ice-cream stand. "How about I treat you to an ice-cream cone?" Nick asked.

"All right, big spender," she said with a smile, "I'll let you buy me a cone."

He'd never enjoyed buying anything for a woman as much as he did that ice cream. Together, they strolled back to the hotel, completely in harmony with each other.

When they reached the hotel, the staff again seemed to almost snap to attention all around them.

Nick responded to those who greeted him calmly, but after they got into the elevator, he said to Julia, "It's almost as if they're hiding something."

"What do you mean?"

"Haven't you noticed how oddly they're behaving?"

"No, I wouldn't. I thought they were always wanting to serve you." She gave him a droll look.

He chuckled. "You're thinking I'm spoiled again, but I promise they don't normally jump every time I come into the hotel. I still think it must be you."

"I'm not doing anything," she protested.

"I think they're all attentive because they think you're beautiful."

Her cheeks flushed. "You're being ridiculous."

"Maybe, but I tell you, something's going on."

When Nick offered to order their dinner brought up to the suite, rather than going down to the restaurant, Julia readily agreed. Whatever was going on with the staff, she now realized it was better not to go downstairs. Besides, she and Nick seemed to be getting along just fine right now.

And maybe Pat would call with the information they'd been waiting for.

"What would you like to eat?" Nick asked her.

"I enjoyed the meal you ordered last time."

"Including the Death by Chocolate? You didn't even try yours last time."

"Maybe you should skip the dessert," Julia said, not responding to his teasing.

He phoned in the order and was told it would be there at six o'clock.

Julia noticed he frowned as he ended the call. "Is something wrong?"

"No, I'm just being silly."

He put down his book, stood and stretched. "I haven't spent such a lazy day in a long time."

"Oh, really? Not even on the weekends?"

"No. Too much to do."

"Does your father have anything to do with the business these days?"

"No."

"Why?"

"He said the world had passed him by. He was afraid he'd hold us back, me and the hotels."

"But he's still so young." Julia stared at him. "Was that his idea, or yours?"

"I thought he should enjoy life. He's worked hard all his life."

"So you take away his profession and you take away his personal relationships? Is he even willing to speak to you these days?"

"Yes!" Nick snapped. Then he stared out the window, as if thinking about what she'd said.

Julia didn't say anything else. She didn't want to be at odds with Nick. She'd enjoyed their afternoon. It surprised her how reluctant she was to lose that sense of well-being.

"I think I'll go take a shower and change before dinner."

She headed for her room.

When she came out half an hour later, it was only a few minutes until six. Nick had changed clothes, too. He was back sitting in his chair, reading.

"No word from Pat?" she asked.

"No. If he calls tonight, it will be later."

She followed his lead and picked up her book to read.

Only ten minutes later, at exactly six o'clock, there was a knock on the door.

Nick opened the door to admit the waiter with their dinner. The young man set the table and placed their meal there, then he turned to Nick. "Sir, the chef didn't have his Death by Chocolate dessert quite ready yet, but if you'll call when you finish dinner, I'll bring it to you at once."

Nick frowned. "Isn't that unusual? Did you have a rush on that particular dessert?"

"Actually we did, sir. But the chef is preparing another cake so you and your lady can have it for dessert."

"All right. I'll give you a call."

The waiter let out a big sigh. "Thank you, sir. The chef was afraid you'd be upset." He gave Nick a grin, then bowed and hurried out of the room.

"Stranger and stranger," Nick said.

"Why do you say that?"

"Normally, once they've sold what has been prepared, they simply tell whoever requests more that they're sold out. But for us, the chef is preparing another cake."

"I told you they spoil you," Julia said.

"Maybe. Come to dinner, Julia."

Julia joined him and over dinner they discussed the books they'd bought. She enjoyed the give-and-take of their discussion. Before she realized it, they had finished their dinner.

"I guess I'd better tell them it's time for dessert," Nick said, getting up from the table.

"We don't really need dessert."

"We do if the chef made it just for us. He'd be devastated if we turned down his specialty."

Curious, Julia asked, "You really worry about his feelings?"

"Appreciation for their work is more important than pay raises. Besides, I have a good staff here. I want to keep them happy." He dialed the phone. "We're ready for dessert now. Oh, of course." He hung up the phone, a strange look on his face.

"Something's up," he explained. "The hotel manager asked if he could come discuss an important issue with me."

"I can go to my bedroom," Julia offered.

"That's not necessary. But whatever happens, just go along with it. I'm not sure what's going on here, but it doesn't feel like a business discussion."

Almost at once, they heard a knock on the door. Nick crossed the room and opened it. His manager was there, along with about thirty employees. He stepped back and gestured for them to enter.

Julia rose, standing by the table, unsure what was going on. Why were so many people pouring into the suite?

"Are we having a group discussion?" Nick asked his manager, Paul.

"Not exactly, but we all wanted to be in on the celebration," Paul said.

One of the last to enter was a man carrying a big gift, wrapped in wedding paper. Several people, including the waiter who had brought their dinner, were clearing the table. Just as they'd put everything away, the man set the box on the table.

Julia was getting worried. Something strange was going on. She moved closer to her bedroom.

"Well, what did you want to discuss, Paul? It must be important if it takes this many people," Nick said.

Before Paul could answer, they all heard the elevator arrive on the penthouse level. Everyone turned expectantly toward the open door.

Julia gasped as a gentleman wearing a chef's hat pushed a cart out of the elevator. On it sat a gorgeous wedding cake, topped with white icing with pastel roses.

Julia stared at the cake, feeling as if things were moving in slow motion.

Nick, too, was staring at the cake.

Paul grinned at Nick. "We hope you don't mind that we changed your dessert order."

"You had a wedding cake left over?" Nick asked in a strange voice.

Julia took another step toward her bedroom.

Paul laughed. "We know you like to keep your life private, Nick. And we promise we haven't told anyone else, but we wanted to celebrate your wedding."

"We all went together to buy you a wedding present. Won't you open it?" one of the women asked.

Nick's gaze met Julia's and she was worried about what she saw in his eyes.

Suddenly, he hurried toward her. Before she knew what was happening, he pulled her into his arms. "They've figured out our secret, sweetheart," he said aloud and then whispered, "Play along, please."

He kissed her and turned them both around to face the crowd. "Allow me to introduce Julia, my wife."

Julia tried to get out a protest before everyone could hear and believe what he'd said, but he kissed her again before she could say anything.

There was applause and cheering.

"Open your gift from us," several people said.

"You have to do this," Nick whispered to Julia.

She turned to the big box. "You shouldn't have done this," she managed to say.

After carefully unwrapping the gift, she discovered a set of Waterford crystal, a service for twelve. Overwhelmed, Julia had to pull herself together to express her appreciation.

"This is gorgeous. So elegant," Julia said, removing one of the glasses to hold it out to the employees.

More cheering. Julia fought back tears as Nick's arm came around her.

"This truly is a generous gift, and much appreciated," Nick told his employees.

"Now the wedding cake," Paul said.

Julia hesitated. "I hope you brought plates for all of you."

The chef bent down to show stacks of plates on the second shelf, along with forks. "But you and Nick must share the first piece."

"Of—of course." Julia took the knife the chef offered and moved toward the cake. Nick joined her. "It's almost too beautiful to cut."

"Wait, I'll take a picture so you'll always remember how beautiful it is," one of the women said.

As she and Nick posed with the cake, Julia struggled to smile. Everything had happened so quickly, and Nick's impassioned plea to cooperate had rushed her into a string of lies.

After they cut the first piece, Julia knew what was expected of her. She broke off a piece of cake and fed it to Nick. He did the same with her, being careful not to make a mess.

Then Julia began cutting pieces for everyone, a very popular move on her part. When she'd finished serving everyone, she cut herself another piece to enjoy, because the cake was delicious. She didn't see any point in being a martyr.

It seemed like a long time before the impromptu party ended. Julia stood beside Nick and shook every hand as they said goodbye and thanked the staff again.

Finally, the door closed and they were alone.

Julia looked at Nick. "What just happened?"

"It was what you warned me about. That couple in the limo believed we'd gotten married and they told someone at the front desk."

Julia drew a deep breath. "What do we do now?"

"We'll be leaving soon. Later, I'll tell them we broke up. That's all."

"Do I get the Waterford or do you?" she asked in a cool voice.

"You can have custody if I get visitation rights," he teased.

Sternly, she looked at him. "This isn't funny, Nick. I'm going to bed."

She started for her bedroom.

"Wrong room, Julia."

"Of course this is my room. All my things are—" Suddenly his meaning registered in her befuddled brain.

He expected her to sleep with him…like husband and wife.

Chapter Eight

Julia didn't allow Nick to speak. She started spewing like a volcanic eruption. "Wait just a minute, Nick Rampling! I went along with those lies because you didn't want to disappoint your people, but I'm not sleeping with you! We're not really married, remember?"

"Of course I remember. I'm not asking you to sleep with me. But we can't use two bedrooms. If we do, when the maids come to clean, it'll be all over the hotel that I can't even bed my own wife!"

"Well, that's not my problem!" Julia snapped.

Nick drew a deep breath. "All I'm asking is that you move your things into my bedroom. I'll sleep out here on the sofa. But I want it to look as if we're...together."

Julia felt bad that she'd accused Nick of trying to make her sleep with him. To make amends, she said, "I can sleep on the couch. I'm smaller and I'll be more comfortable on it."

"I don't think so. I'm responsible for the situation, and I'll sleep on the sofa. Now, can you move your things into my bedroom?"

"Yes, of course." Julia hurried into the room she'd been using and gathered her things. She made sure the room looked untouched when she left it. "Do—do you want to take a shower tonight or in the morning?"

"I'll take my shower in the morning," Nick said. "I'll just need a pillow and a blanket."

Julia took one of the pillows off the bed and a blanket from the closet. "Are you sure you don't want me to sleep on the sofa?"

Nick came to take the pillow and blanket. "I'm sure," he said, before he bent down and kissed her again.

"Stop that, Nick. We shouldn't— We had to earlier, but not now."

"Sorry, it got to be a habit." But she noticed the smile he tried to hide. "I think I'll go to bed now, if you have everything you need."

"Sure, unless you want another piece of cake."

"No, thank you." She entered the bedroom and closed the door. Then she leaned against it, letting a sense of relief wash over her. She'd managed to escape from Nick without letting on how much she'd enjoyed his kisses.

* * *

Nick tried reading for a while, but he couldn't shove Julia out of his thoughts. He had to admit that he wanted her. He wanted to make love to her, to share the events of the day with her. He stopped short of admitting he wanted to share his life with her.

He wasn't that crazy.

Picking up his book, he tried again to lose himself in a world where Julia didn't exist.

The phone interrupted his efforts.

"Pat! I'd given up on you calling this evening."

"Sorry to call so late, Nick, but I finally picked up their trail. They've flown to Hawaii."

"When?" Nick asked.

"The same day they married. They flew back to L.A. and connected to a flight to Honolulu."

"They've been moving fast."

"Yeah, this lady must really be tempting."

Nick immediately pictured Julia. "Yes, I suppose she is."

"So, are you going to Hawaii?"

"Yeah. First thing in the morning. Thanks, Pat."

"No problem, Nick. If you need more help, just give me a call."

He hung up the phone just as the door to his bedroom opened. Julia paused there, looking more like a child with her big eyes than a woman who stirred his blood.

"Was that Pat?"

"Yeah. We're heading to Hawaii in the morning. Ever been there?"

"Hawaii? No, never. Are you sure?"

"Pat said they flew back to L.A. the same day they got married and connected with a flight to Hawaii."

Julia sighed. "Okay. I'll get my credit card."

"I can't use your card, honey. Remember, everyone here thinks we're married. I'll pay for the flight and you can pay me back."

"All right, but no first class. I can't afford that."

Nick grimaced. "I suppose I can bear coach."

He picked up the phone and called the desk downstairs and requested two seats on the next flight to Hawaii. "Ten o'clock? Yes, that'll be fine. Try to get us two seats on the side. We don't want to be in the center. Yeah, let me know. Oh, and you'd better make Julia's flight in her maiden name. She doesn't have ID yet showing our marriage."

After he hung up the phone, he looked at Julia. "There's a flight at ten tomorrow morning. They'll let me know if they get us two seats on it, so we'll need to be up early in the morning. We'll probably need to be at the airport by eight-thirty."

"So I guess I'd better get some sleep while I can," Julia said with a sigh.

"Yeah, I'm afraid so. I'll get you up at seven in the morning."

She disappeared again, and he lay back against the sofa. Good thing they'd bought some books today, because they had a long flight ahead of them.

And he needed to keep his mind occupied with something other than Julia.

* * *

When Nick got the wake-up call the next morning, he struggled to get up. After all, he hadn't gotten much sleep during the night. And he had an ache in his back that could be attributed to the division of the sofa cushions.

When he managed to stand, he grabbed his pillow and blanket and opened the door to the bedroom where Julia was peacefully sleeping under the covers. He didn't think he'd ever seen such a sweet sight.

Stowing away the blanket in the closet, he circled the bed to restore the pillow to its rightful place, before he shook Julia's shoulder.

She shrugged off his hand, snuggling deeper into the covers.

"Julia, it's time to get up. But if you don't mind my taking a shower first, you can stay in bed until I get out. Okay?"

"Mmm."

He thought that was a yes. He gathered what he needed and shut the door behind him.

Julia stirred at the sound of the shower. It must be time to wake up. She hadn't gotten enough sleep last night. But something important was supposed to happen this morning. Something connected with her mother. What was it?

Gradually, reality returned. Oh, yes. She was flying to Hawaii this morning to find her mother and her new husband. With Nick.

It seemed she'd already heard him this morning. Then the shower intruded into her consciousness. Who was in the shower?

Then she remembered why she was sleeping in Nick's room. He must've gotten into the shower while she was sleeping.

Julia slipped out of bed and put on her robe. She didn't want to lie in bed waiting for him to emerge. In the living room, she saw the remainder of the cake. She cut herself another piece and was eating it when Nick entered the room.

"Having more wedding cake?" he asked.

"I just hate to see it go to waste. It really tastes good. You must tell your chef how much I like it."

"I will. In the meantime, you'd better get in the shower, because I intend to eat a real breakfast."

Julia grinned. "I get the message, sir," she said with a mock salute. Taking her last bite of cake, she hurried to the bedroom.

When she emerged half an hour later, she not only was dressed to leave, but she also had packed her bag. "Quick enough for you?"

"Great. Let me just throw my things in my bag, and we'll go downstairs to eat. Do you know what you want? You can call down and preorder for us so it will be ready when we get there."

"We can do that?"

"My hotel, remember?"

She picked up the phone. When the coffee shop attendant answered, she started to identify herself as Julia Chance. But she suddenly remembered her new identity. "Uh, this is Julia Rampling in the penthouse. My h-husband and I will be down in about five minutes. We would both like to order now so it will be ready when we arrive. We're on a tight schedule today."

"Certainly, Mrs. Rampling."

Julia ordered, then hung up the phone. Not only was Nick spoiled, but Julia was becoming that way, too. It would be hard to return to her small home in Houston, to live alone and have no one to wait on her. Until now she hadn't even thought that her mother might move to Kansas City, where Abe lived, now that they were married.

She would miss her mother. They visited each other several times each week and often had phone conversations. Her moving to Kansas City would leave a hole in Julia's life.

"I'm not a mama's baby," she muttered to herself just as the bedroom door opened.

"Were you speaking to me?" Nick asked.

"No! No, I was talking to myself. Are you ready?"

"Yeah. Let's go."

Julia took a last look at the elegant suite of rooms. She would miss the time spent here.

"Why do you look so sad?"

Julia hurried past Nick, not wanting to answer that question. She rushed into the elevator, carrying her bag. Nick looked at her, but she avoided his gaze. They rode down in silence.

When the elevator door opened, a bellhop was

waiting to take their bags. "I'll place them in the limo, sir."

"Thanks, that would be great." Nick gave him their bags and then took Julia's hand. She tried to pull away, but he quickly reminded her of their "marriage" before he led her to the coffee shop.

"Good morning, Mr. and Mrs. Rampling. Your breakfast is ready. This way, please."

They slid into their booth and the waiter set down their breakfasts, including coffee and juice. Julia smiled gratefully and Nick thanked the waiter.

"I'll certainly miss the service you get here," Julia murmured.

Nick nodded. "We pride ourselves on our service."

When they'd finished, Julia once again left a hefty tip.

"You're going to spoil Jim," Nick said. He put his hand on her back to guide her to the door leading to the front driveway where James was waiting. Several of the staff came over to bid them goodbye. Julia shook their hands and thanked them again for their thoughtfulness.

When they got into the limo, she hurriedly whispered, "What about the Waterford?"

"They're going to ship it home."

"So I guess I don't get custody after all," she muttered.

"I forgot about that. Maybe I can ship it to you after I get back home."

"No, I couldn't accept it. Besides, I'm sure it'll fit into your lifestyle more than mine."

"We'll worry about it later."

They rode in relaxed silence the rest of the way to the airport.

After they got out, they thanked James and made their way to the counter, where they picked up their tickets.

It didn't take long before they were on the plane. Nick looked longingly at the first-class seats as they passed on their way to the second row of coach. Nick rationalized that at least they would be served faster than those in the back of the plane. It wasn't first class, but it wasn't bad, Nick decided.

"You want the window seat or the aisle seat?" he asked Julia.

"I'll take the window seat, if you don't mind."

"No, that suits me. Did you bring your books to read?"

"Yes, of course. You did, too, didn't you?"

"Sure. I'm planning on trading with you after I finish mine."

She smiled at him as she slipped into the window seat. He sat down beside her. "You know, we're turning into comfortable traveling companions. It's lots more fun than traveling alone."

"At least you're getting something out of this," she said, looking out the window.

"Aren't you getting anything out of our adventure?"

"Yes, as long as I don't remember what's going to happen when we find them."

"Julia—" Nick began, frustration in his voice.

"Never mind," Julia said. She opened her book. "I'm going to start reading. That way I won't get nervous when we take off."

"Feel free to hold my hand, if that helps."

She shrugged her shoulders. "I'll just read. I think that'll take care of it."

Nick pulled out the book he'd begun the day before. But he didn't read much, because his attention was too focused on Julia. She hadn't mentioned her fear during takeoffs before now. Was it because of the long flight?

As the plane pushed away from the gate, Nick noticed that Julia's fingers were clutching her book so tightly, they were turning white.

He pried her left hand off the book and held it in his. "Julia, it's going to be all right."

"Of course it is. There's no need to hold my hand."

"I thought I might warm it up a little. Feels like a chunk of ice." He was prepared for her response. She immediately tried to withdraw her hand from his grip. He held on tightly.

"Let go, Nick! I didn't ask you—"

She stopped abruptly as the plane began its takeoff. Her eyes widened, and she held on tightly to his hand.

"Did I tell you Pat gave me the name of their hotel in Honolulu?" he asked, hoping to distract her at least a little.

"D-do you have a hotel in Honolulu?"

"Nope, sorry, I don't. We'll both be regular customers."

"I'll miss that special service your hotel provides to its owner," she said with a shaky grin.

"Me, too. I've thought about buying a hotel in Hawaii, or maybe even building over there, but then I'd be making this trip a lot."

She shuddered. "I don't think that would be worth it."

"It's not that bad occasionally, but I wouldn't want to make the trip every three months."

She looked at him, aghast. "Definitely not! Is that how often you visit your hotels?"

"I usually try to pop in once a month, but I don't think I'd make a trip to Hawaii every month."

Nick noticed a little warmth in her fingers again, and he was relieved. "Don't you ever fly for your job?"

"Teaching second graders? No, of course not. Our lives are completely different, Nick. I couldn't do what you do."

"The more you fly, the more comfortable you become," he said. "I would've thought by now you'd think nothing of it."

She was losing the heat he'd felt in her fingers. Suddenly they were cold again. "No, I don't fly all over the place, or stay in great hotels or have a lot of money to spend. First class is your style, not mine."

"I bet you could fly better if you put your mind to it."

"I—I can't help it! I've told myself it's irrational,

but—but I think it's because we're flying over water. A lot of water." She looked out the window.

Nick knew they were already over water.

"Tell you what, why don't you take a nap. You probably didn't get enough sleep last night, right?"

"Right, but I don't think I can go to sleep."

"I think you can if you'll let me help you," he said gently.

"How?"

"Let me hold you. You'll feel safer, more secure. When you wake up, you'll feel better."

Without waiting for her agreement, he pulled her against him and wrapped his arms around her. "Close your eyes, honey, and just rest. Everything's going to be all right."

To his surprise, she buried her face against his chest and let out a long sigh. The tension in her body slowly seeped out. He felt her fall asleep against him.

He loved holding her against him. He didn't bother trying to read again. He just held Julia. Then he closed his eyes and rested his head on hers.

"Sir, I'm sorry, but I thought you might like your lunch. You don't want to go the entire flight without a meal."

At the flight attendant's words, Nick stirred and Julia's eyes popped open. She found herself wrapped in Nick's arms. Even as she remembered why she was in that situation, she straightened and removed Nick's arms.

"I—I definitely want my lunch," she said, smiling at the flight attendant.

"Put down your tray and I'll serve you at once."

As they always were in coach, the tray was on the back of the seat in front of her, and Julia quickly lowered the tray.

"You have a choice of chicken fettuccine or meat loaf."

Julia chose the chicken.

"And you, sir, get the meat loaf."

"I don't have a choice?"

"No, we've passed out all the other meals. We let you sleep as long as possible."

"Okay, I guess I'll have the meat loaf."

"I can switch with you," Julia offered.

"No, honey, I'd have chosen the meat loaf. It works out fine." He looked at the meal in front of him. "And I can always finish up with the chocolate cake."

Julia smiled. "We do have a history with chocolate cake, don't we?"

"Yeah, we do."

"Thank you for helping me relax, Nick."

"I think it helped me relax, too. I didn't expect to go to sleep. But we managed to sleep a good three hours, almost half the flight."

"So it will just be like the flight to L.A.?"

"Sort of. Will it be worth the effort?"

"I—guess so, but I don't think I'd choose to make this trip again."

Chapter Nine

When the plane landed on Oahu three hours later, Julia let out a big sigh. Back on dry land. She felt like kneeling and kissing the ground, but she feared everyone would think she was crazy.

Instead, she gracefully received a lei as she exited the Jetway into the airport.

"You look very festive," Nick whispered to her.

"So do you. It's not just a girl thing here. How far is it to the hotel?" she asked as they boarded a mini-van.

"Depends on the traffic."

"Traffic here in Honolulu? I thought this was supposed to be paradise."

"Sometimes paradise gets very crowded. Everyone chooses paradise for their honeymoon, you know."

"You mean they get married and then get on a plane for at least six hours?"

"Not to your taste?" he teased.

"I wouldn't want to— Never mind. Oh, look, I can see the ocean!"

"You like it better since you're on dry land?"

"I should've never let you know what was upsetting me!"

"Surely we're friends by now Julia." He took her hand in his.

"It would be nice to think that, but I can't be your friend when you're determined to ruin my mother's life." She pulled her hand away.

Nick started to ask her how she could sleep in his arms if they weren't friends. But he didn't want to push her away. He enjoyed being near her too much.

"It'll all be over soon, honey. We'll talk to them as soon as we get to the hotel. But you know what? I'll miss you once everything is settled."

She wouldn't let his comment affect her. She deflected it and said, "I'm sure you'll quickly recover."

The van halted and the driver came around to open the door for them. "Welcome to the hotel," he said in an island accent.

Julia gave him a brief smile as she stepped out. Then she waited for Nick.

He got out and stopped beside her. "Ready?"

"Of course."

They walked into the hotel and registered, using separate credit cards, of course, which won her a speculative look from the woman behind the desk.

Nick asked the clerk, "While we're here, we're looking for our parents, Mr. and Mrs. Abe Rampling. Can you tell us what room they're in?" He threw in his most charming smile.

While Julia was sure the woman appreciated his good looks, she shook her head. "I'm sorry, we're not allowed to pass out room numbers."

"But can you tell us if they're registered?" Nick stared at her with his dazzling blue eyes.

"Yes, I can do that. Just a moment." She moved away to type on another machine.

Julia tensed, knowing that if they found the couple, her mother would suffer at Nick's hands. Nick, however, appeared nonchalant, which irritated Julia.

The woman returned to face them. "No, sir. They are not registered at this time."

"But they *were* registered here?" Nick asked, frowning.

"Yes, sir, for one night only. Then they flew to the big island to our hotel there."

"So when can we make the same flight?"

Julia stepped a little closer.

"There's a flight each morning, and a return flight in the afternoon."

"Can you book us on the flight in the morning?"

"Of course. For two?"

Both Nick and the woman looked at Julia. She swallowed, wishing she could say no. Instead, she nodded.

"One moment, please." She punched more keys before jotting the information on a piece of paper, which she handed to Nick. "The flight leaves at ten o'clock tomorrow morning. Our van will be happy to take you to the airport."

"Great. Thanks." Then he took Julia's arm and led her to the elevator.

"I think I could find the elevator without your guidance," Julia whispered.

"Probably, but I don't want to take any chances."

Their rooms were on separate floors, so Julia was confused when Nick got out on her floor. "What are you doing? This isn't your floor, is it?"

"No, I'm one up. But I wanted to see you to your room. And we need to make plans," he added.

"Plans for what?" Julia asked, stopping to look at him.

"For dinner. I don't want to eat alone. Do you?"

"I—I guess not." Julia was afraid she'd made a mistake. She knew by now she wasn't going to talk Nick out of his intentions. She didn't want her mother to think she agreed with him. Somehow, since they seemed much closer to the newlyweds now, she had to worry about things like that.

"Can't we just eat in the hotel?"

"We can, but there's this great restaurant right on the beach."

"On the beach? I'm not sure it sounds sanitary."

"I thought it sounded romantic," Nick said.

"Romantic? Why would either of us want to enjoy a *romantic* evening?" Julia was horrified by that idea. She already felt guilty about the time she spent with Nick.

Nick shook his head. "Look at it as an educational event. Believe me, dinner on the beach in an elegant restaurant is really great."

"What do they serve? Because I'm not that fond of fish."

"Don't worry, sweetheart, they'll have something you like." Nick bent down and kissed her.

"Nick, there's no need to kiss me. We aren't in your hotel in L.A. No one needs to believe we're married now."

"Oh, yeah, I forgot. I'll make reservations and give you a call," he said as Julia opened the door. Then he followed her into the room.

"Does this suit you?" he asked. "Is it big enough?"

"Nick, I'm just one person. I don't need that much room."

"I tried to rent a suite, but they didn't have any available. Now call me if you want to go out and look around. I can take you."

"Nick, it's paradise, remember? I'll be fine."

"I'm sure you will, but I'll feel better if you don't go out on your own. The buddy system is always best."

"Go to your room, Nick. I'll be fine."

"Just call me if you change your mind," he repeated as he went out the door. Julia shut it after him.

She couldn't believe how protective Nick had become. It's a good thing he hadn't been able to rent a suite. She thought she needed some separation from him. It was too easy to lean against that strong man, rely on his muscular arms. She was used to being on her own. Since that was her present state, she'd better not forget how to manage by herself.

She crossed over to the balcony and opened the glass door. A gentle breeze wafted into the room. She stepped out and watched the waves roll onto the beach below. Maybe those honeymooners had the right idea.

Taking some money out of her purse, along with her key, she walked down the hall to the soda machine and got a Diet Coke to take back to her room. Opening the drink, she took it to the balcony and curled up on the chaise longue. She wanted to relax a little and the sound of the waves soothed her.

Nick couldn't believe that Julia had immediately gone out by herself after he had warned her not to. What was wrong with the woman? Didn't she know how many predators there were out there, just looking for a woman by herself?

Hanging up the phone, Nick paced back and forth several times. Then he grabbed the phone again.

A few minutes later, he'd convinced the desk to send a bellhop to Julia's room, where Nick would be. The bellhop would go into her room to be sure she hadn't fallen and hit her head.

If she wasn't there, he was going to wait at her door to catch her when she came in.

When the bellhop arrived, Nick was already waiting. The bellhop knocked on the door and called Julia's name, but there was no response. He inserted the key into the door and opened it.

Nick brushed past him, checking the bathroom for Julia. He almost missed the slight opening from the glass door, but some of the gentle breeze was flowing into the room. Nick stood there, his hands on his hips. There she was, Sleeping Beauty. He hadn't thought she'd be tired since she'd slept so much on the plane.

Obviously, he was wrong.

He indicated her position to the bellhop and told him not to awaken her. Then, after writing a quick note and leaving it by the phone, he followed the bellhop out.

When they reached the hallway, with the door closed behind them, the bellhop said, "Sir, if you don't mind my saying, she's going to know you were in her room when she finds the note."

"Not a problem. I'll explain how worried I was."

Now more than ever, he wished he'd been able to rent a suite. He'd feel better having access to her. But it was only for one night. When they got to the big island, they'd have different arrangements.

He'd make sure of that.

"Are you sure I'm going to like dining on the beach?" Julia asked on their way to dinner.

"You liked listening to the sound of the waves from your balcony, right?" He didn't wait for her answer. "And that's why I think you'll like your dinner."

"Maybe."

When they reached the restaurant, the maître d'

showed them out the door to the beach. Julia was sold at once. They had a silklike tarp on top of the sand and the table was draped in beautiful linens. A striped awning covered the dining area.

Julia sat down, totally enthralled. A beautiful bowl of flowers, fragrant and colorful, was in the center of the table. The maître d' handed them their menus and assured them their waiter would be right with them.

"Well, I'm impressed so far. I'm sorry I doubted you, Nick."

The waiter appeared immediately. "Good evening, sir, madam. May I bring you a drink?"

"Oh, no, I—"

Nick cut her off. "Yes, please, we'll take two virgin papaya drinks."

When the waiter left, Julia said, "Nick, I really don't want the drink."

"Won't you trust me again?"

"I guess so. Until you make a mistake," she said with a smile, enjoying the light evening breeze.

"Wow! Such pressure!"

"Yes, I can tell you're really worried," she teased.

Nick leaned back in his chair. "How do you feel about Hawaii now that we're here?"

"It's very nice, but I do feel a little funny about being on a small island surrounded by all that ocean."

"You're just a land lubber, aren't you?"

"I'm afraid so," she said with a sigh.

The waiter delivered two tall glasses with a yellow liquid in it.

Julia picked hers up and took the straw in her hand. "Here goes," she said with a nod in his direction. Nick didn't look worried.

After one sip, she knew why. "Oh, my. Are you sure these are legal?"

Nick's smile broadened. "I'm sure."

"I might make a meal just of this."

Nick leaned forward. "That's because you haven't looked at the menu."

"I'm feeling another 'trust me' coming on," Julia said.

"You're right. I've eaten here a number of times and I've never been disappointed."

Two hours later, when they rose from their table on the beach, Julia had no complaints. It had been a lovely evening. It also rated high on the romance quotient. A golden moon rose from the sea about halfway through the dinner. As it rose, it turned to silver and lit the waves as they crested off the beach.

As they left the restaurant, Julia sighed.

Nick caught her hand. "Nice evening?"

"A wonderful evening. Thank you."

"My pleasure," Nick said and lifted her hand to his lips.

She twisted her hand away. "The romance part of it doesn't apply to us, remember? We're on different sides of this argument."

"We don't know that until I meet your mother."

"Sure. That's why you've made such a determined push to find her. Because you're dying to offer them your blessings!"

"I have to be sure, Julia. Surely you can understand that. My father's been taken before. My stepmother was a first-class gold digger."

"I'm sure you're right, but that doesn't mean you can assume every other woman will be the same."

"Can't I?" In front of the hotel, Nick stopped abruptly, and his voice thickened. "My father isn't the only one. Did you wonder why I haven't married? I almost did once. But I overheard her telling her girlfriend what a jackpot she'd discovered. I sent my attorney to inform her that I no longer wanted to marry her. She settled for fifty thousand dollars."

Julia felt a twinge in her heart for the pain he'd suffered, and the betrayal. "I—I'm sorry, Nick, but surely you realize that doesn't mean every woman will be like that, thinking only of money."

Nick shook his head. "You just don't get it. You, and possibly your mother, may be the exception to the rule. If I asked you to marry me and then I heard you talking about how you could rip me off, would you take money in a settlement?"

"No, of course not, but I wouldn't say something like that. If I agreed to marry a man, it would be because I loved him. There'd be no price to pay me for his not keeping his word."

Nick held open the door to their hotel for Julia. They walked to the elevator in silence. Other guests also entered the elevator, so the ride up was silent.

Julia stepped out on her floor and discovered Nick right behind her. "You don't have to see me to my door, Nick," she said.

"Yes, I do. We're in the middle of an important discussion."

"I don't think we'll ever agree."

"Maybe not, but I've got to give it a shot. You're condemning me for wanting to protect my father, and yet that's the very reason you're here, isn't it?"

"Yes," Julia agreed as she opened her door. She already knew Nick was coming in. "But I trust my mother to make the right decisions for her life. I just want to protect her from the shock of what you're planning to do."

"So what if you're wrong about your mother. What if she refuses to sign the prenup?"

"Why should she? Abe is her husband."

"Because if she refuses, both my father and I will know she married him for his money."

"So you have no belief in your father's decisions?"

"You haven't met the women he's dated in the past."

"I know about your stepmother, but—"

"Honey, that doesn't begin to tell you about my father's efforts to find a new love. I've paid off eight women, all of whom were delighted to accept my offer."

"Eight?" Julia asked, shocked. "Isn't that a little hard on your budget?"

Nick laughed. "That's why I love you, Julia. You're an intelligent young woman, but you're also a little naive."

Julia stiffened. "I don't appreciate that remark."

"Want me to apologize?"

"No, but I think our conversation is over. We lead different lives, Nick. We have nothing in common and never will. You can go to bed now. I'll see you in the morning."

"Not yet. You agreed that all I'm doing is protecting my father. Which is what you're doing for your mother. So why is what I'm doing so bad?"

"Because you don't trust your father."

"Would you, after nine mistakes? I have to find out why they got married."

"Maybe that's what upsets me the most. You don't believe in love!"

"You know what upsets me about you?"

"What?" Julia asked sharply.

"You believe in something that you've never experienced."

Julia's eyes filled with inexplicable tears. She turned away from him. "Just go, Nick."

"Honey, I'm not trying to hurt you," he said, taking her shoulders in his hands.

She twisted out of his hold and walked to the glass door, staring out at the ocean.

Julia closed her eyes, hoping it would keep the tears from falling. She felt Nick come to stand behind her, but he didn't touch her.

"Julia, I'm trying to explain why I'm doing what I'm doing. I'm not being cruel, trying to protect Dad from that kind of woman. Don't you think he'll be happier with someone who doesn't value money over romance? If your mother won't take a payoff, maybe they'll have a happy marriage. I even hope that they will, but I'll admit I don't think it will happen."

"Fine, Nick. Just leave me alone." The tears were starting to fall now. She didn't want him to see them.

"I'll go, as soon as you look at me and tell me again to go."

"Fine!" She swung around, ignoring the tears as she said, "Please go, Nick! Go away and leave me alone!"

Nick pulled her against him and covered her lips with his.

His action was totally unexpected and left her breathless. She pushed away. "No!" she gasped.

"Sweetheart, what's wrong?"

"I couldn't breathe! Besides, you shouldn't— I mean, you weren't supposed to kiss me anymore."

"I wasn't supposed to make you cry, either."

"I've stopped crying, I promise."

"Do you understand a little better why—"

"Yes, I understand." She took a step backward when he moved toward her. "No, Nick, just go."

"But you're going with me in the morning?" He bent down to look her in the eye. "Right?"

"Yes, Nick, I'll go with you in the morning. After all, I've come all this long way to protect her."

"Good girl. I'll see you for breakfast, okay?"

"Yes, of course."

"I think we'd better eat about eight-thirty. Do you need a wake-up call?"

"I can arrange that on my own, Nick."

"All right. I'll see you then."

When she finally got him out of her room, she leaned against the door and let out a deep sigh. Yes, she understood him. But they weren't even close to being alike.

And her poor heart was suffering.

Chapter Ten

Nick was waiting for her the next morning in the coffee shop. He'd already ordered breakfast for both of them. Maybe he'd ordered hers as a promise to himself that she would show. He'd paced the floor for a long time last night, hoping and praying that he hadn't convinced her to abandon their pursuit of their parents.

When he saw her at the coffee shop door, he practically leaped from the booth he was in to make sure she saw him. "Julia, over here." He felt like a fool because that was the first time he'd pursued a woman, hoping she'd join him. How had their roles been reversed?

"Good morning," he said as she sat down.

"Good morning, Nick."

Her voice hadn't echoed his enthusiasm.

"Is everything all right?"

"Yes, of course," she said, her gaze on the table.

The waiter arrived just then with their orders.

Julia stared as he set a plate full of pancakes and bacon in front of her, with a small glass of orange juice and a hot cup of coffee. The same meal was being delivered to Nick. "You ordered for me?"

"Yeah, I thought it would save time for us. We don't want to miss the plane."

"Thanks." She picked up a bacon strip. "Why do you think they went to the big island?"

"There are several beautiful resorts over there. The one connected to this hotel is supposed to be very special."

"You've been there?"

"Yeah. It was a couple of years ago and—"

"And you didn't go alone, I'd guess."

"No, but that doesn't matter."

"Did your father come along and buy her off?"

He put down his fork and met her eyes squarely. "Julia, I may have brought a companion for my trip, but that's all she was, and I made that clear."

"Oh, I see."

But it was clear she didn't approve. With a sigh, he said, "Eat your breakfast, Julia."

They had no more conversation until they were in a minivan with a group of people leaving on the ten o'clock flight to the island of Hawaii.

"How big is this plane?" Julia asked.

Nick didn't like the look of fear on her face. "I'm

sure it'll be safe. After all, they make the flight twice a day."

He could tell he hadn't convinced her.

When the minivan pulled up at the airport, Nick took Julia's hand, and she didn't even fight the gesture. They followed the others to the appropriate gate where a jet was pulled up.

"It looks rather small."

"That should make it more safe. There's less weight to hold up. By the way, did you notice the palm trees all over the island?"

She gave him a disgusted look. "Do you really think the palm trees are going to distract me?"

He grinned. "I thought I'd give it a try."

"You'll have to do better than that if you want me to forget that we're going to fly over the water today."

"Does your mother hate flying over water?"

"No. At least, I don't think so. I don't really know because we haven't flown over water before."

"You know it's all in your head, don't you?"

"Maybe so, but that doesn't mean I can just dismiss it. It won't go away."

As if to reinforce that thought, the gate attendant announced, "We are now ready to board flight number six for the big island at this time."

Julia stiffened.

"Give me your hand, honey. I'll be right beside you, I promise."

Though she did as he said, she muttered, "I feel like such a baby."

"Think about seeing your mom again. You'll be glad to see her, won't you?"

"Yes."

Not an enthusiastic start, but at least it was a start.

The plane had two rows of seats going down the plane, each two seats wide. Nick found their row and seated himself beside the window. "I think it will be better if you don't look out while we're flying."

"Maybe you're right. I'll just concentrate on reading my book."

The takeoff was smooth and Nick thought they would have a smooth ride.

He opened his book, just like Julia, and started reading. About fifteen minutes later, the pilot came on the loudspeaker. "Folks, we're going to experience a little rough weather, but we should land right on schedule in half an hour. Hopefully that half hour won't be too uncomfortable for you. Please be sure your safety belt is fastened."

Julia's eyes widened and she glanced out the plane window. They were on the east side of the plane, and the sky appeared clear.

Nick glanced out the west side and almost gasped. It was turning black on that side of the plane. He ducked his head in his book, hoping Julia would do the same. She followed his lead until they hit the first air pocket. The plane dropped sharply. Several passengers screamed and a flight attendant who had not belted herself in yet fell, which didn't help anyone's nerves.

The copilot came out of the cockpit to assist her to her seat and be sure she wasn't injured. Then, he headed back down the long row, trying to appear calm. He, too, almost fell when the plane hit another air pocket.

They had numerous rocky movements in the air. Once, it appeared lightning would hit the plane, but narrowly missed. Julia was clinging tightly to Nick's hand.

"Do you see land yet?" she kept asking him. With the cloud cover increasing, he wondered if they'd see land until they were five feet above it.

When they finally did reach the big island, they made a rough landing but rolled up safely next to the gate.

"There we go, Julia. See, we got here safely," Nick said as he helped Julia disembark. He thought they'd made it just fine until Julia bent over and lost all her breakfast. Nick held on to her, and a flight attendant gave her a wet towelette.

"Th-thank you," Julia told the woman. "I'm so sorry."

"Don't worry about it. People get airsick even on good days. Today, I'm particularly surprised we didn't have more illness after what we just flew through."

"That's so kind of you," Julia said in a weak voice.

Nick helped her into the airport and found the van to take them to their resort.

He wasn't sure if they should register or not. He thought they should first find out if their parents were staying there.

When they reached the resort, he settled Julia in

a comfortable chair in the reception area where she could, hopefully, regain her strength while he figured out where Abe and Lois were.

He inquired with the clerk at the receptionist desk. She looked at the computer and said, "They were here a few days ago, but they didn't stay. They cancelled their reservation. I remember they decided to go back on the afternoon flight. Such a nice couple."

"Yes, I'm sure they were." He stood there for a moment, trying to decide what he should do. He hated to tell Julia that they were on another wild-goose chase set up by his father. Or that they would have to get back on that plane. But he had to do both. "Ma'am, can I make a reservation for two on the return flight this afternoon?"

"Of course, sir. It leaves at 3:00 p.m."

After he had them scheduled on that flight, he walked back to where Julia was sitting in the comfortable chair. "Uh, sweetheart—"

"Don't tell me! They're not here!"

"No, they're not," he said apologetically.

"Damn it, Nick! Where are they? Did they return to Oahu? Why didn't Pat tell us that?"

"I don't know, but I'm going to ask him right now."

Sitting down beside Julia, he called Pat on the cell phone and explained what had happened.

"They didn't? Yeah, well, we've got to start asking. Yeah, start checking the flights. My dad is setting traps for us and so far we've fallen into every one of them.

"Okay, okay. Yeah, we're headed back to Oahu this afternoon. Would you make us a hotel reservation? Yeah, I'd like a suite. Great, thanks, Pat."

He flipped his cell phone shut and looked at Julia, who was now lying against the chair, her eyes closed. "Julia, you want to get something to eat?"

"How about a walk along the beach instead?" she suggested.

Nick stood at once and offered a hand to help her up. "That will be great. Come on, we'll—"

He stopped talking when lightning flashed outside the hotel and a huge roar of thunder followed. Then the skies opened up and rain poured down.

Nick and Julia stared at each other.

"Maybe not a walk on the beach," Nick said ruefully. "But at least we'll get rid of the storm before it's time to start back."

Julia came to an abrupt halt. "Maybe I haven't been understanding, but do you mean we have to get back in that little plane and fly back to Oahu today?"

"Come on, Jules, it wasn't that bad," he said heartily, all the time knowing she'd thought it was hell.

"What did you just call me?" she asked, intensity in her gaze.

He blinked several times. "I called you Jules. Why?"

"Never mind. What do we do now?"

"I'd suggest the restaurant before it fills up. Everyone else will figure out that's all there is to do pretty soon."

"Okay," she agreed, but it was obvious she was struggling with the idea of eating again.

"We could start off with some hot tea," he said.

She perked up at that suggestion.

They found a table in the restaurant and Nick ordered a pot of hot tea for Julia, since she'd said she'd try tea, and a cup of coffee for him.

The tea helped settle Julia's stomach. After a few moments, she agreed to order some lunch. Outside, the rain was still pouring down. The sea also appeared to be fairly angry. Julia shivered.

"Are you cold?" Nick asked.

"No, I was just thinking about flying back to Oahu."

"We won't go if the weather hasn't calmed down," he promised.

"I don't want to hold us up," Julia said.

"So far we haven't found a new place to look. I can't believe my dad has been so sneaky."

Julia pressed her lips tightly together.

Nick cut off any chastising remark about how he'd brought it on himself. "Don't say it."

The waiter brought their order.

"You might as well eat slowly," Nick said.

They did so, and he worked hard to keep a conversation going.

It wasn't as easy as it had been in the past. She was more resistant to building a rapport. He suspected she soon would refuse to speak to him at all.

As they got closer to the time of departure for the commuter plane, the storm didn't abate.

Julia kept staring out the window.

"I'll go check on the flight, honey. Just wait here."

Julia watched him go.

"Are you talking about the flight back to Oahu?" a lady at the next table asked.

Julia looked up in surprise. "Yes, we are. Are you on that flight?"

"We were supposed to be on it, but my husband just heard they've canceled it. You'd better go ask for your room back. They're filling up quick."

Julia stared at her. "Filling up? What do you mean?"

"They're running out of hotel rooms. People are going to have to camp out in the lobby."

Just then, Nick came back in, and Julia looked up at him anxiously. "Have you heard about the flight?"

"Yeah, it's been canceled. We'll be stuck on this island for the night."

"That lady said the rooms were filling up."

"Right. I got the last one."

Julia froze. "The last *one?*" she said faintly.

"It has two beds, Julia. I'll be a gentleman."

"Don't worry. I can stay in the lobby. The lady said a lot of people will have to stay there for the night."

"But we got a room, Julia. There's no need for you to sleep in the lobby."

"It's all right. I'll be fine."

"No, you won't." He stuck his hand in his pocket and slapped the key down on the table. "Take the room, Julia." Then he got up and walked out of the restaurant. Julia wanted to go after him, to explain her concerns, but she knew she couldn't. How could she tell him it wasn't only him she didn't trust, but herself, as well?

Instead she paid the bill and went to the front desk. "I need a room," she said.

"I'm sorry, ma'am, but we have no more rooms. You're welcome to use the lobby to be comfortable."

"Thank you," she finally said and walked away— through the very lobby where Nick would be spending the night.

When she entered the room that Nick had registered for, she stared at it. It had two full beds, a lanai and a sitting area. Nick was right. They could share the room. She'd just have to keep herself under control. After all, it was only for one night.

Nick had put his suitcase in the chair where he'd be spending the night. He stood beside it, his back to the rest of the lobby, watching the storm as it engulfed the entire island.

It was a shame, really, since Julia had never been to the big island. She wasn't seeing it at its best. And he was willing to bet she wouldn't want to fly over water to visit again.

He turned back to the chair with a sigh. He guessed he'd have a chance to finish his book this evening. There wasn't anything else he'd be able to do.

He tried to find a comfortable spot in the chair, but it was futile. Just as he was considering stuffing the chair with a couple of dirty T-shirts, he looked up to find Julia standing beside the chair.

Before he could say anything, Julia said, "Will you forgive me?"

"For what?"

"For not trusting you. We may not agree on certain things, but you've never lied to me."

"I appreciate your saying that, Julia. But just because I don't lie doesn't mean you have to trust me in a bedroom alone with you."

"Yes, it does. Please come share the bedroom with me."

Nick was trying to decide what to do when the man next to him said, "I'll be glad to share with her if you don't."

Julia gave him a wide stare.

Nick immediately picked up his bag. "Lead the way, Julia."

Once they were in the elevator, he said, "You wouldn't have let him share with you, would you?"

"No. But I thought it worked well forcing you to make a decision," she said with a grin.

When they got to the room, Julia chose which bed she wanted and Nick took the other. "I thought maybe we could play cards or something like that for a while."

"Good idea. I have a deck of cards in my suitcase," Nick said.

"Great. Do you play gin?"

"Sure. Are we playing for pennies?"

"I…guess," she said slowly. "A penny a point?"

"Works for me," he said.

They moved to the sitting area and played on the

coffee table. Three hours later, Nick said it was time to settle up.

"Let's see, you have 755 points and I have 400. I think I owe you 355 points, or 355 pennies."

"I think you've more than paid your share." Julia stood and stretched. Then she looked out the window. "Look. The rain stopped."

Nick joined her at the window. "For now but those clouds still have a lot of water in them."

Julia shivered. "I'm very glad you got us a room."

"Me, too, but if at any point you change your mind, I'll leave."

"No. I trust you."

Nick took a deep breath. "Yeah. Well, that pretty much limits what we can do."

She looked a little shocked, and he laughed. "Yeah, amazing, isn't it?"

"What do you mean?"

"You just put me on my honor. That means I can't betray your trust."

"Did you intend to? I said I trusted you."

"I know, but three hours alone with you and I needed a reminder."

"Maybe we should get out of the room. Is it dinnertime?"

"Close enough. I'll call and see if I can get a reservation for us."

Julia walked out on the balcony. The island was beautiful, but she still felt anxious about being here. Once she had found her mother, she intended to go back to the mainland and never return.

Nick joined her on the lanai, looking relieved. "We got a reservation in half an hour. Then they're showing a movie at eight o'clock. I think that would be a good deal. It'll occupy us with something other than each other."

"Sure," Julia agreed. "What movie?"

"It's a classic, *What's Up, Doc?* I think it stars Ryan O'Neal and Barbra Streisand."

"I've never seen it."

"I've heard it's funny. We could use a little fun to-night."

When they went down for dinner, the restaurant was crowded, and Nick and Julia shared a small table over in a corner. But the food was as good as before and Julia began to relax again.

They finished eating just a few minutes before the movie began. Julia excused herself to go freshen up and Nick looked for good seats in the ballroom-turned-theatre. Nick waved to Julia as she came to the door of the ballroom.

"This was very smart of the hotel to have some-thing like this to occupy all their extra guests," she said as she sat beside him. "Otherwise, they'd be overrun with kids not having anything to do."

Julia paused. "Do your hotels have an emergency plan?"

"Not like this one," Nick admitted.

"We don't know how good this one is until we've seen the movie," Julia teased.

Nick agreed with her.

Until lightning struck again and the lights went out.

Chapter Eleven

"Please remain seated," a voice in the dark said. "We'll have lights back in just a minute."

Nick reached over and found Julia's hand. "You okay?"

"Yes, as long as I'm not on a plane flying over the ocean," she told him. It felt good to laugh about that paralyzing fear.

They both heard movement.

"What can they do?" Julia asked.

"If they're smart, they have a generator to provide power to part of the hotel."

"I hope you're right."

As if Julia had spoken the magic words, the electricity came back on.

"Sorry for the delay, folks," the man up front said. "Now, let's get started."

Two hours later, when the movie ended, Nick had his arm around Julia and she was leaning on him. When the lights came on, bringing them back to reality, Julia moved away from him. She had to be careful. It was too easy to fall for his charm.

"Well, that was fun, wasn't it?" she asked.

"Yeah. You want some dessert before we go up to bed—I mean, to our room."

"No, I'm not hungry."

"Right. Why don't you go on up and get ready for bed. I'll be up in a few minutes."

She didn't hesitate to take him up on his offer, and she really appreciated it. After all, there wasn't much for him to do to occupy his time. But he knew she'd like some privacy.

When Nick tiptoed into the darkened room, with only the bathroom light on, Julia pretended to be asleep. Once he made his way into the bathroom and closed the door behind him, she breathed a sigh of relief. For a while anyway, there'd be a barrier between them.

When morning came, one would think there had never been a cloud in the sky, Julia thought. The island glistened in the bright sunlight. After dressing in the bathroom, she opened the lanai and settled on the chaise longue and let the sun wash over her.

Half an hour later, Nick awoke and called her name.

She looked over her shoulder and answered him. "What's wrong?"

He drew a deep breath. "I thought you'd left without me."

"Not likely. Whose hand would I hold on the flight?"

He grinned. "Good point. I'll get dressed. Then we can get some breakfast."

While he was in the bathroom, his cell phone rang so Julia answered it.

"Who is this?" asked a deep male voice.

"This is Julia Chance. Nick is unavailable at the moment. May I help you or have him call you?"

"This is Pat Browning."

"Oh, yes, of course, Mr. Browning. I'll get Nick."

She knocked on the bathroom door. "Nick, Pat Browning is on the phone."

Nick opened the bathroom door at once. He took the phone. "You got something, Pat?"

"No, that's the frustrating part."

"Wait, I'll put you on speakerphone."

"Nick, I can't find any trace of your dad. He's not registered at any Hawaiian hotels and I don't show that he's bought any airline tickets. It's like he's disappeared. Would he have enough cash to get off the islands?"

"I don't think so. You haven't found any withdrawals of cash, have you?"

"Nope. Any ideas?"

Julia sat there listening. Suddenly, she had an idea. "Pat, it's Julia. Look under the name of Lois Chance. She may have bought the tickets for wherever they've gone."

"Good thinking. That didn't occur to me because— Never mind."

"I don't think that's likely," Nick said.

Julia knew why the two men thought as they did. Because Abe's women had never paid for anything. But Nick and Mr. Browning had never met her mother.

Finally Mr. Browning agreed to check. "Well, it won't hurt to look. I'll have an answer before you get back to the mainland."

"No, Pat, today we're just getting back to Oahu. We had a storm yesterday and couldn't get out of here last night. Check to be sure they held our reservations for us."

"Will do. Call me when you're in your hotel room on Oahu."

"Okay."

After Nick put the phone away, he said, "You shouldn't have suggested that."

"What? That Mom might've paid for some tickets?"

"Yeah."

"But it's the answer. With your feelings about Mom, it's the last thing you'd look for. That's why it's so obvious."

"Dad always pays for everything. He wouldn't expect that."

Julia looked at him. "I guess we'll see."

"Come on, Julia. We can't start arguing before breakfast. I think there's a law against that."

"I'm not arguing. I just said we'll see."

After an enjoyable breakfast, Nick suggested they go for a swim in the ocean, since their flight didn't leave until three.

Julia immediately declined.

"Why? Are you afraid of the ocean? I thought you just didn't like to fly over it."

"I said no because I don't have a swimsuit."

"They have some in the shop."

"No, Nick, I told you about hotel shops."

"I looked at everything in that blasted store last night while you were up in the room. They have some reasonable suits."

Julia followed him to the hotel shop and discovered he was right. And since she never intended returning to Hawaii, she decided it would be worth the price for a once-in-a-lifetime opportunity.

Although Nick teased her about her conservative swimsuit choice, they were soon on the beach, enjoying themselves. Nick was a perfect companion, letting her try different things, but always making sure he was there to catch her if she fell. After their swim, they stretched out on the chairs provided and stared at the magical playland they'd been enjoying.

"It is gorgeous here, isn't it?" she said dreamily as she stared at the beach.

"Yes, it is, but if we're going to catch our plane, we'd better head upstairs and get changed."

Julia looked at her watch and gasped. "We'd better hurry or we won't have time for lunch."

"We could stay another day, if you want," Nick said, not looking at her.

"No," she responded, but the regret in her voice was audible.

"Why not?"

"Because I'm not here on vacation. I'm here to find Mom."

That reminder seemed to put a damper on the rest of their time there. Even their lunch was silent and hurried.

And, admittedly, the closer it got to flight time, the more tense Julia became.

She withdrew even more from Nick. When they settled in their seats on the plane, she wouldn't even hold his hand. "No. I'm going to be fine. It's silly to give in to such weakness."

They had a smooth flight, much to Julia's relief, and were soon back at the hotel on Oahu. This time, they had a suite available. Nick immediately took it, in spite of Julia's protests.

When they reached their suite, he pulled out his phone and called Pat. Putting him on speakerphone, he asked the all-important question. "Did you find anything?"

"I sure did. Your dad's going all out this time."

"Where did they go?"

"To Bora-Bora."

Julia gasped. "You're sure?"

"Yeah, your mom bought the tickets and they're registered at the Lagoon hotel under her name also. That was a great suggestion, you had, Julia. Nick and I were too close to the problem to even think about your mother paying for them."

"Thanks for the compliment, Pat."

"Pat—" Nick began and then stopped. "Never mind. Get us two tickets for the next flight."

"You're on a flight leaving at eight o'clock tonight."

Nick thanked him and hung up.

"We've got a couple of hours before dinner. What do you want to do?"

"Why don't we call them instead of flying down there?"

He looked at her skeptically.

"You just want to warn your mother about why I'm coming."

"No, I don't. I have more faith in my mother than you have in your father."

"That's not true."

"Then my calling them isn't a problem?"

"As long as you don't tell your mother to sign the prenup so she can continue to dupe both me and my father."

Julia gave him a sad look, but she accepted his ground rule.

"Fine. I'll call her right now and you can hear our entire conversation."

"Okay, fine," he agreed, a touch of steel in his voice.

Nick got the number of the hotel. She dialed the number, excited by the prospect of finally getting to talk to her mother.

When the hotel operator answered, she asked for Lois Chance's room. "One moment, please."

"Hello?"

Julia would've recognized Abe's voice anywhere because it sounded so much like Nick's. "Abe?"

"Yes?"

"I'm Julia Chance. May I speak to my mother?"

"Yes, of course, Julia. She's been anxious about you. By the way, I'm looking forward to meeting you."

"Me, too, Abe."

When her mother's voice came on the phone, Julia suddenly sat down, tears filling her eyes. "Mom?"

"Oh, honey, how are you? How did you find us?"

"Well, when you weren't in Hawaii—" She paused. Then she said, "Never mind, it doesn't matter. How are you?"

"Oh, I'm wonderful. Abe and I are married and— You don't mind, do you? I know your father wouldn't mind, but are you okay with it?"

"Of course I am, Mom, as long as you're happy."

"Oh, yes. Abe and I are perfect for each other."

Julia heard the bliss in her mother's voice and was satisfied.

"I'm glad you found each other. Are—are you going to move to Kansas City?"

"Yes, but Abe's house is big. He said you could move with us."

"No, Mom. You and Abe should be on your own. But we can talk often, and you and Abe can come back to Houston every once in a while to visit."

"Or you could come to Kansas City."

"We'll see. I just wanted to make sure you were

safe and happy. I'll see you when you get back to—when you come for all your things."

"Of course, dear."

"All right. I love you, Mom."

"I love you, too."

Julia hung up the phone and sat there, not moving.

"Well?"

Nick's voice shook her from her thoughts. "You heard the call. I didn't say anything to tell Mom what was in store for her."

"How was my dad?"

Julia gave him a curious look. "He sounded fine."

"Was he upset that you found them?"

"He didn't sound like it. He said he looked forward to meeting me."

"Hmm. He must not have made the connection," Nick said under his breath.

Unless the man was senile, it was the opposite, Julia thought. She didn't think her mother would be so enthralled with someone who couldn't remember his own son. But Abe could. That much was obvious by the way they'd traveled. Still, she kept silent.

"Well, at least you'll see your mother tomorrow."

"No, I won't."

Nick stared at her. "Of course you will. We'll get there in the morning and we'll see them at once."

"I'm not going to Bora-Bora with you."

"Why not? I thought you wanted to protect your mother."

"I don't need to anymore."

"Julia, you're not making sense. You traveled a long way to make sure your mother is safe. Why stop now, just short of the goal?"

"Because I've achieved my goal. My mother is safe and happy on her honeymoon. She doesn't need me. I don't think she did all along. My faith in her wasn't strong enough. But it is now."

"Then come along for the ride. You've never seen Bora-Bora, have you?"

"No."

"Well, then come see it. It will be my treat to you for coming with me."

"Thanks for the offer, but no."

"So you're going to stay here and have a vacation?"

"No, Nick. It's over. I'm going home."

He said nothing at first, and looked... Was that disappointment she saw in his eyes? "Are you going back through L.A.? I can call the hotel and—"

"No. I'm flying straight to Houston. I've traveled too much. I want to go home."

She picked up the phone and called the airlines to find out when the next flight to Houston left.

"Six-thirty? Yes, a seat for one." She gave her name and her credit card number.

After she hung up the phone, she found Nick standing at the glass door, staring out at the waves.

"Nick, my flight leaves at six-thirty."

"I heard."

"I guess I should go to the airport. They like you to be there early."

He turned to look at her. Then he said, "I'll take you."

"I can go by myself, Nick. I'm not a baby."

"I know. Unless you're flying over water and there's a storm."

She gave him a smile. "I'm praying there's no storm tonight."

"Me, too."

"I guess we didn't need the suite after all."

"No, I guess not."

She intended to make a little speech about how kind he'd been to her, but she decided to save it for the airport.

She took her bag and started for the door. He picked up his and followed her to hold open the door.

Downstairs, he paused by the desk, presumably to tell them they were leaving and to pay for the suite. Then he took Julia's arm and they went out front. He hailed a cab and put both their bags in the trunk. "Seems like we're setting out on another adventure, doesn't it? Only this time we're both going off by ourselves."

"Yes." She fought back the tears that filled her eyes when she thought about leaving Nick. They had come a long way from their first hostile meeting.

But she knew she was doing the right thing. Her mother was happy and no amount of money would separate her from Abe. She knew that, but Nick would have to make that discovery in his own way.

When they reached the airport, Julia purchased her ticket and found a seat in the waiting area. Nick remained at her side.

"I'm fine now, Nick. You can go."

"No, I can't. I have to see you on your plane. Then I'll go find my flight."

They sat in silence. Occasionally, he'd make a comment, or she would, about some of the passengers around them. Otherwise, they sat silently. She felt his warmth next to her and didn't want to lose it. In fact, she admitted to herself, she didn't want to lose him, either. She'd done the worst thing she could've done—she'd fallen in love with Nick.

All this time, she'd been waiting to find the man who would make her happy for the rest of her life, and she'd found him, in the worst possible place.

Now she couldn't go to Kansas City to see her mother because she might run into Nick. She couldn't spend Christmas with her mother and Abe because Nick would be there. She couldn't do anything without running into Nick except stay at home and teach second graders.

What was wrong with her? She loved her job.

But she wouldn't see Nick.

With a sigh, she closed her eyes.

"What's wrong, honey? Are you worried about the flight?"

She was glad he had asked that question, instead of realizing her heart was breaking. "Yes, a little."

"Tell you what," he said, standing. "I'll go get a ticket on this flight and go with you. Once you're home, I could come back and talk to Dad and your mother."

"No, Nick!" Julia reached out to clutch his hand.

"Don't be ridiculous. You'd be going in the opposite direction from them. That would be crazy."

"I don't like you flying by yourself. You'd be more comfortable if I'm with you."

"Nick, we can't do that. I have to go home by myself. We both know that."

"Are you sure?"

"I'm sure," she said sadly. She also prayed the time would pass quickly. She couldn't stand long, drawn-out goodbyes.

"I don't have your phone number," he said, sitting down. "Give it to me and I'll call you after I—I've visited our parents."

She gave him her phone number. "But you really don't need to call me. I know things will be all right."

"You're that sure?"

"Yes. My mom loves your dad. No amount of money will change her mind about that."

There was another long silence after that exchange. Finally, Nick took her hand in his and held it.

When her flight was called, she stood. Nick did, too.

She stared at him, memorizing his face. "I want to thank you for all your kindnesses to me. We were a great traveling team."

He nodded. "Yes, we were, weren't we?"

She nodded and turned to go. She had to before she burst into tears.

But he didn't let her go. Spinning her around, he kissed her. Not a casual, goodbye kiss, but a lover's kiss.

When he released her, she muttered her goodbye and rushed for the plane. She was too afraid he'd see her tears if she turned to look at him again.

So she saved her tears until she was on the plane.

She never even noticed the water below her. She was too busy crying as she flew home.

When the plane set down in Houston, Julia expected to feel relief that her hectic traveling was over.

But even being at home couldn't make her forget her loneliness and her mother's interview with Nick.

She believed her mother would come through it successfully, but she didn't think she would.

She could never forgive Nick if he dismissed her mother's love for Abe and broke up their marriage. And if that happened, she could never see Nick again.

What was she thinking? Either way, she would never see Nick again.

Chapter Twelve

Nick couldn't figure it out.

All the eagerness, determination, intense feeling of a disaster had left him. His father had married Julia's mother—and Nick thought it might be the best thing his father had ever done.

As long as Lois was like her daughter.

Julia was…Julia. She'd only gotten better the longer he'd known her.

Tonight, when he'd watched her hurry onto the plane, he'd worried about her flying alone. He should've gone with her to make sure she made it home all right. His dad would've expected that of him.

Instead, he was on his flight to Bora-Bora. A long flight. Oh, how he wished Julia were beside him.

He'd tried reading his book, but he couldn't share interesting parts with Julia. He'd thought about sleeping, but he couldn't cuddle with her, feel her warmth against his skin.

He finally took out the deck of cards they'd used to play gin. Playing solitaire was mind-numbing, but at least he wouldn't think too much about Julia.

Finally, he slept for a few hours. After all, he needed to be able to make sense in the morning. When he awoke, the plane was landing in Bora-Bora and the sun was up.

Bora-Bora was even more lush than Hawaii, or maybe less tamed. He couldn't decide. But he knew Julia would like it. Once again he wished she had come with him.

The closer he got to meeting his father's new wife, the more worried he became. He'd never see Julia again if he broke up Abe and Lois's marriage.

He discovered his father and Lois were in a bungalow separate from the main hotel. A young native woman showed him to the front door of their cozy, thatched bungalow, then, with a nod, she walked away.

Taking a deep breath to shore up his suddenly shaky nerves, Nick knocked on the door.

It was opened by an older version of Julia—the same slender build, the same blond hair, though shorter to frame her face, the same blue eyes. Lois Chance had aged well. "Yes?" she asked.

"Lois, I'm Nick. Is my dad here?"

"Oh, Nick, welcome." Lois smiled as she threw

her arms around his neck. "I've been so anxious to meet you."

"Thank you, Lois," Nick said. He felt a warmth rising in him.

"Nick." His father's voice was almost as welcoming as his new wife's.

Lois moved back and Nick crossed the room and hugged his father. "Dad, how are you?"

"Better than I can ever remember. How are you?"

"I'm good."

"We've been expecting you."

"You have?"

"Yeah. If Julia could find us, we figured you couldn't be far behind."

His father moved across the room to put an arm around his new wife. "I told Lois you'd come here. She didn't really believe me."

An awkward silence fell on the room, one Nick felt compelled to end with an explanation. He took a deep breath. "I don't know if my father has told you about his past."

"He said he made a bad marriage after your mother's death."

"Yes, that's true, but he's shown a talent for finding…well, the wrong kind of woman. Several times I've paid off the women who gladly accepted the money and went away."

Lois gasped, staring at Nick. "That's—that's awful. Oh, poor Abe," she said, burying her face in Abe's chest. Much as Julia had done when she was frightened on the plane ride to the big island, Nick realized.

"Son—" Abe began.

But Nick continued, "Usually I ask them to sign a prenup, and they're pleased to at least get some money out of it."

"Well, that won't be the case here. I'll gladly sign your prenup."

Nick frowned. "I didn't intend to offer it."

"Good," Abe finally interjected. "Lois is not like the rest of them!"

"I realize that, Dad."

"Abe, sweetheart, why not let me sign the prenup? I don't want there to be any doubt in Nick's mind about my feelings for you. We can share my money."

Nick grinned at his dad. "So, you found a lady who is independently wealthy, did you?"

"She's not wealthy. She got some insurance money after her husband's death."

"Do you have more?" Lois demanded, her dander up.

"Yeah, sweetheart, I do. We—" he looked at his son "—we own the Rampling Hotels." Abe watched his wife carefully.

"Abe Rampling! You lied to me!" She stared at her husband and Nick, anger on her face. "How dare you!"

"Lois, why are you upset?" Nick asked.

"I don't like being lied to!" she snapped.

"Honey, I was afraid to tell you. I didn't want you to pretend to like me because I could buy you things." Abe tried getting close to her again, but she pushed him away.

"How can I ever trust you again, Abe?" She

walked away from him. "How do I know you haven't lied to me about other things?"

"I haven't, Lois, I promise! Ask Nick. I'm usually very honest."

"That's true, Lois. He is always honest. And he never believed any woman would lie to him, either, which is why he got into trouble."

"I don't lie, either! Do you believe me, Abe?"

"Oh, yes, honey, I believe you and I always will," Abe promised, pulling her into his arms again.

This time she went to him willingly. "Okay, Abe, we'll forget this happened," she said, her hand on her husband's cheek.

Abe—and Nick—breathed a sigh of relief. Until Lois spoke again.

"So you can put his money away and we'll live off mine."

"No!" both men shouted.

"But it's the only way we can be sure, Abe, both of us."

Nick tried to reason with her. "Lois, it's obvious you didn't marry Dad for his money. Suppose he had a bad illness that required a lot of money. If he couldn't get to his money, he might deplete yours and leave you penniless. He'd be devastated by that."

"But doesn't he have insurance?"

"Yes, of course, but—"

Abe stopped him. "What if Julia decided to get married? I'd want to pay for the wedding and send her on a nice honeymoon. I couldn't do that if I couldn't get to my own money."

"But she's not your daughter, Abe."

"I have a feeling I'm going to want to think she is. Why don't we just be married and share everything, like we planned all along?"

"But I wouldn't be bringing as much to the marriage as you," Lois protested.

Abe leaned down and kissed her. "Oh, honey, I've been looking for someone like you for most of my life, and I'd give all my money to be married to you. It's just not necessary."

"That's such a nice thing for you to say, Abe."

"It's the truth, sweetheart."

"Nick, do you feel like that?" Lois asked.

"Oh, yeah," he said fervently. But Nick was thinking of more than his father's marriage. He was thinking of Julia, and how everything his father said was true of his feelings for her.

Abe stared at his son. "Do you feel all right, son?"

"Uh, yeah, sorry. I was distracted for a moment."

"Why don't we all go have lunch in the hotel? I can get to know Nick, and I'll tell both of you about Julia." Lois took their agreement for granted as she picked up her purse and took Abe's hand.

When they reached the restaurant, Nick had realized he'd have to tell Abe and Lois about all his travels with Julia. He suspected she'd be honest with them when they got back to the mainland.

The waitress took their orders and left the table. Before Lois could begin talking, Nick said, "There's something I have to tell you both."

"Yes?" Lois asked eagerly.

Abe looked worried.

"I already know Julia."

"How could you know Julia?" Lois asked, confused.

"She's been— I mean, you've dated her?" Abe asked.

"No!" Nick hurriedly replied. "I—I met her while I was looking for you at the Hotel Luna."

Lois gasped. "Julia went to the Hotel Luna? Oh, no! I didn't think she'd come after me. We chose the Hotel Luna for you to—I mean—"

"I know why, Lois," Nick said wryly. "And I'm not saying I didn't deserve it. But it almost caused Julia some trouble. Thank goodness she didn't get out of the car she'd rented."

"Then how did you find her?" Abe asked sternly.

"I got her to give me a ride because my taxi had abandoned me."

"She allowed a stranger into her car with her?" Lois asked in horror.

Damn, this was going from bad to worse. Skipping the dangerous details, he glossed over their days together. "Anyway, we flew together to L.A. to find you. And Las Vegas. And Oahu and Hawaii. That's when she called you."

"You were with her?"

"Yeah. We'd planned to fly to Bora-Bora, but she decided to call. After the call, she flew home to Houston."

"You didn't take advantage of her, did you?" Abe demanded.

"No, Dad. She's a younger Lois," he said, knowing his father would understand. Just as Lois wasn't one of Abe's gold diggers, Julia wasn't one of Nick's babes. She was a forever kind of woman.

"You're serious?" his father asked in surprise.

Nick nodded.

"How serious?"

"Just like you, Dad," Nick said. "If she'll have me."

"Wait! What are you talking about?" Lois asked.

"I've just explained to my father that I feel about Julia the same way he feels about you."

"You love Julia?" Lois asked in amazement. "Oh, that's wonderful!"

"I hope Julia thinks so."

"You didn't ask her?"

"She was traveling with me to find you. I didn't think I should say anything when she didn't feel she could leave. That wouldn't have been the thing to do."

"Oh, Nick, you're wonderful!" Lois said, leaning over to kiss his cheek.

"Want to play another set?" Julia asked her friend as they met at the net.

"No!" Marissa answered forcefully. "What are you trying to do, kill me?"

"Oh, come on, it's not that hot." Julia looked around to find another victim.

"You're not going to find anyone else crazy enough to come out in the heat of the day to play tennis," Marissa said. "What's up with you?"

"Nothing. I'll buy you a bottle of water since you say I worked you so hard."

"I'll take you up on that." Soon they were seated at a table with an umbrella to offer some much-needed shade. They each had a glass with ice and water.

"Really, what's up with you, Julia? You mysteriously disappear for several weeks and you haven't been the same since. What happened?"

"Mom got married."

"She did? That's good news, isn't it?"

"Yes, of course. But she's moving to Kansas City. I'll miss her."

"Well, of course you will, but Kansas City's not that far away. You can visit her a lot."

"Maybe."

"That's not all that's bothering you, is it?"

Julia laughed, but even she couldn't hide the sadness in her voice. "I guess not."

"Well, aren't you going to tell me?"

"It's hard to explain. But basically, I fell in love with the wrong person. Someone who doesn't believe in love."

"Oh, no! Are you sure?"

She gave a sad nod. Then she tried changing the subject. "What about you? How's your summer going?"

"Better than yours. Mac and I have been talking about setting a date."

"Congratulations! I'm very happy for you, Marissa."

"Thanks. Mac just has to get up the nerve to talk with my dad. I told him that's not a problem. My parents already know I love him. But he insists that's the way it should be done."

"That's sweet. He's a good man."

"Yes, he is. Why don't I ask him if he has any single friends I haven't met? We could double-date."

"Thanks, Marissa. Maybe in the fall. I need some recovery time." Maybe the rest of her life. Julia didn't want to think about that.

After she returned to her home, she showered and changed, just twisting her hair on top of her head, instead of styling it.

It had been five days since she'd left Nick in Hawaii. She'd thought he would have called by now. But he hadn't. Nor had her mother.

She was fighting self-pity. After all, Nick hadn't invited her to fall for him. Of course, he had kissed her. But most of those kisses had been casual kisses. Only the last one, at the airport, had been one she couldn't forget.

She sighed and flopped down on her sofa, reaching for the remote control of her television. But she didn't feel like watching TV. Nor did she want to read. Every time she picked up the book she'd bought in L.A., she thought about Nick and the afternoon they'd spent in the suite of the L.A. hotel, where the employees thought they'd gotten married. And the party they'd had that evening.

Julia wiped away a tear. She couldn't start crying again. She'd done too much of that since she'd gotten home. She was suffering from a loss, like the death of a loved one.

But she must get it under control.

The doorbell rang, and Julia made sure she'd wiped another tear away before she looked through the peephole. Then she stepped back, staring at the door.

It couldn't be… Was it a dream she'd conjured in her wakefulness?

The doorbell sounded again, and she finally opened the door. "Hi, Nick."

"Hi, honey. How are you doing?"

"Fine. And you?"

"I'm fine. Are you going to invite me in?"

"Yes, of course— Wait. Are Mom and Abe still married?"

"Yes."

"Then you can come in."

"Thanks."

She moved back and allowed him in. Then she directed him toward the living room where they sat opposite each other.

"Very nice," Nick said.

"Thank you. Did you just get back from Bora-Bora?"

"I got back a couple of days ago. I intended to call, but then I had to come to our Houston hotel, so I thought I'd just drop in."

Nick was playing it casual, so she adapted the same tone. "How was Mom?"

"Fine. She's a lovely lady, like her daughter."

"Thank you. Did you ask her to sign the prenup?"

"No, but she offered."

Julia glared at him, vindicated. "Well, I hope you were satisfied."

Nick shook his head. "It almost gave Dad a heart attack."

"What are you talking about?"

"Your mom got upset when she found out Dad had lied to her."

Julia felt almost as upset as her mother had. "What did he lie about?"

"Apparently he'd never told her about his money."

"Well, I guess it would be a shock to learn that he had more than her."

"Julia, how much did your mom get in life insurance?"

"A little over two hundred thousand."

Nick smiled. "Yeah, we have a little more."

Julia's chin shot up. "It's not nice to brag about your money."

"Oh, sorry." He looked contrite. "By the way, your mom didn't point that out."

"So, you approve of Mom?"

"Oh, yeah. And Dad finally convinced her to accept his money."

Julia stared at him. "He did?"

"Yeah. He made a nice speech about how long he'd been looking for someone like her."

"I'm glad they're happy."

"Oh, but they're not."

Julia jumped to her feet. "They aren't? Why? What did you do, Nick?"

"Well, you know how I always promised to be honest?"

"Yes, of course."

"I told them I'd been traveling with you as my companion. I mentioned sharing the suite at the L.A. hotel, and about our 'wedding reception' and—"

"Nick, you didn't! Surely you explained—"

"I tried, Jules, really I did. But they insisted we get married!"

Julia sat down as her knees collapsed.

"What—what did you say?" she asked faintly.

"They insisted we get married. Your mother said nice girls didn't travel across the country with strange men."

She stared at him. Then she burst into laughter. "Okay, I can take a joke, Nick, but you went too far with that statement."

"I did?"

"Definitely. My mother didn't say something so ridiculous."

"You mean she thinks it's okay if you travel the country with strange men?" He crossed his arms over his chest and leaned back against her sofa.

"What are you up to?"

"What do you mean?" he asked.

"Why are you teasing me like this?"

He leaned forward, catching her hands in his. "Because I'm afraid if I'm serious, you'll send me packing. I've never asked anyone to marry me when I'm shaking with fear." He laughed nervously. "Actually, I've never asked anyone to marry me period."

Julia stared at him, her mind unable to process anything he was saying. As if he were speaking in an ancient tongue, she didn't understand a word. Or maybe self-preservation had kicked in and her brain simply refused to understand.

Whichever it was, she pulled her hands away and sank away from him. She was too close, too afraid she would throw herself at him if she let down her guard.

"Does the idea of marrying me disgust you so much?" he asked.

So he was talking about marriage? She thought she'd heard that word.

"No, of course not!" she replied. "But there's only one reason to marry. And it's not impropriety or convenience. And it's definitely not money." No it was only love. The kind of love she felt for Nick.

The kind of love he didn't feel for her.

She blinked furiously to hold back the tears that threatened to fall.

"Tell me what the reason is," Nick said to her.

"You already know, Nick." She lost the battle and the tears ran freely down her cheeks.

"Don't cry, honey." Without saying anything else, he pulled her into his arms. "I shouldn't have done it that way. I'll admit it was because I was afraid you wouldn't believe me."

Through her tears, she asked, "What are you talking about?"

He held her at arm's length and looked directly into her blue eyes. "I love you, Jules. So much. And

I want to marry you and be with you for the rest of our lives."

Julia simply stared at him, unable to speak. He had proposed to her... He loved her.

"So Julia, will you marry me?" he repeated.

"You're serious?"

"Yeah. I've missed you ever since you got on that damn plane and flew away from me. I didn't even want to go to Bora-Bora, but I felt I had to be sure." He shook his head and laughed. "You know what your mom did when I introduced myself to her?"

Julia answered without hesitation. "She hugged you."

"How did you know?"

"Because that's how she is."

"Yeah, just like her daughter." He gave her another kiss then, just like the one at the airport, and she felt it down to her toes. "You feel so good, honey."

"So do you. I've missed you, too, Nick. And I love you."

"When did you figure it out?" he asked, as if he couldn't help but get all the details.

"That night on the big island when we shared the room."

"Damn, if I'd known, we would've only used one bed."

She swatted him gently on his arm. "I wouldn't have agreed to that!" she exclaimed. Then she smiled. "Well, maybe..."

"Too bad we have a lunch date right now," he

whispered. "We could make up for lost time." He captured her lips again, kissing her deeply as he held her close against him.

When she could breathe again, Julia asked, "What did you say?"

"I said we have a lunch date, one we're already late for."

"With whom?" Then she gasped. "Mom? She's here? Where is she?"

Nick smiled at her reaction. "She and Dad are at our hotel, waiting for us."

"Nick, you beast! Why didn't you tell me?"

"Because I was afraid you'd want to go see your mother and you wouldn't listen to my proposal."

As if that would ever have happened, she thought. She wrapped her arms around his neck. "I may be excited to see Mom, but I'm most excited to know you love me."

"So you want to stay here and make love instead of having lunch?"

"As tempting as that might be, I think I'll choose lunch. Since I've waited all these years, I think I'll walk down the aisle having earned the right to wear white."

"So you'll marry me?"

In all the excitement, all the kissing, she'd forgotten to tell him. "Yes, Nick Rampling, I'll marry you. Forever."

Epilogue

"**I**'m going to have to disappoint Nick," Julia said to her mother over lunch at the Rampling property in Houston.

Lois looked up, surprised. "Why, dear? Everything is going so well. I didn't think you'd like giving up teaching, but Abe says the staff loves having you here and you're getting to know all their employees since you travel so much with Nick."

For the past few months, after their wedding, she'd accompanied Nick on all his trips. Now she was more than just his "companion"—she was his wife. And she'd gotten over her fear of flying over water, too.

"I'm going to have to cut back on my travel schedule soon, Mom."

"Is something wrong?"

Julia leaned in closer. "You promise not to tell Nick?"

"Of course, dear."

"Well, I went to the doctor today." She smiled at the worried look on her mother's face. "And he told me pregnant women shouldn't fly so much in the later months."

Lois erupted in excitement. "You're pregnant? Oh, I'm so happy! When will the baby be born?"

"I'm only two months along, Mom."

"I know, but Abe will be so excited! And I'll be a grandmother!"

"Sh, here come our men," Julia warned.

Nick and his father slid into the empty seats and kissed their wives, scarcely interrupting their conversation long enough to apologize. "Sorry we're late, honey," Nick said.

"You're just in time. We ordered for the two of you. What are you discussing?"

"Dad came up with a great idea for the hotels. We were just discussing the details."

"Good for you, Abe. Nick's been telling me how much help you've been giving him."

For the past few months, Abe had been giving more and more of his time and advice to his son, and Nick seemed happy to have his father back in the business. Abe still had a lot to offer.

Nick clapped his father on the back. "It's true, Dad. We make a good team," Nick said. He turned toward Julia and she could see the concern in his eyes. "How did your appointment go this morning?"

Julia had told Nick nothing about her suspicion of being pregnant. As far as he was concerned, she was looking for the cause of her fatigue of late. She had intended to tell Nick the good news that night, when they were alone, but she couldn't wait another moment to reveal her secret. "Everything's fine."

"Are you sure?" Nick asked quietly, concern in his voice.

"Yes, Dr. Haviland said I was remarkably fit for a pregnant woman."

Abe jumped up to congratulate her, while Lois once again beamed. Nick, however, sat in his chair, looking confused.

"What are you saying, Julia?" he asked.

Abe replied in her stead. "She's saying I'm going to be a grandpa."

Nick stared at her. "Really? We're having a baby? That's why you've been so tired? Is that normal?"

Julia smiled. "Absolutely. The doctor said I should take naps when I'm tired."

"I haven't been asking too much of you, dragging you on all my trips?"

"You know I love going with you," she assured him. "But I'll have to cut back on them when I get bigger."

"I'll cut back, too. Dad and Lois can do a few of the trips. You won't mind, will you?"

"Of course not, Nick," Abe agreed, patting his son on the back.

Nick wasn't really listening. He was busy kissing his wife and telling her the day he'd met her had been the best day of his life—until now.

"Wait until you meet your child, sweetheart. It only gets better from here."

"I'll drink to that," Nick said after another kiss. He started to order champagne all around, but Julia told him she couldn't have alcohol. "Oh, of course not. Orange juice all around," he ordered.

When they lifted their glasses, he said, "To love. The most important thing in the world."

Everyone at that table agreed with him.

* * * * *

If you enjoyed what you just read,
then we've got an offer you can't resist!

Take 2 bestselling love stories FREE!

Plus get a FREE surprise gift!

Clip this page and mail it to Silhouette Reader Service™

IN U.S.A.	IN CANADA
3010 Walden Ave.	P.O. Box 609
P.O. Box 1867	Fort Erie, Ontario
Buffalo, N.Y. 14240-1867	L2A 5X3

YES! Please send me 2 free Silhouette Romance® novels and my free surprise gift. After receiving them, if I don't wish to receive anymore, I can return the shipping statement marked cancel. If I don't cancel, I will receive 4 brand-new novels every month, before they're available in stores! In the U.S.A., bill me at the bargain price of $3.57 plus 25¢ shipping and handling per book and applicable sales tax, if any*. In Canada, bill me at the bargain price of $4.05 plus 25¢ shipping and handling per book and applicable taxes**. That's the complete price and a savings of at least 10% off the cover prices—what a great deal! I understand that accepting the 2 free books and gift places me under no obligation ever to buy any books. I can always return a shipment and cancel at any time. Even if I never buy another book from Silhouette, the 2 free books and gift are mine to keep forever.

210 SDN DZ7L
310 SDN DZ7M

Name	(PLEASE PRINT)	
Address	Apt.#	
City	State/Prov.	Zip/Postal Code

Not valid to current Silhouette Romance® subscribers.

Want to try two free books from another series?
Call 1-800-873-8635 or visit www.morefreebooks.com.

* Terms and prices subject to change without notice. Sales tax applicable in N.Y.
** Canadian residents will be charged applicable provincial taxes and GST.
All orders subject to approval. Offer limited to one per household.
® are registered trademarks owned and used by the trademark owner and or its licensee.

SROM04R   ©2004 Harlequin Enterprises Limited

If you enjoyed what you just read,
then we've got an offer you can't resist!

Take 2 bestselling love stories FREE!
Plus get a FREE surprise gift!

SILHOUETTE *Romance*

COMING NEXT MONTH

#1806 A TAIL OF LOVE—Alice Sharpe
PerPETually Yours
Marnie is a wire fox terrier with a mission: reunite his family.
With strategically placed canine chaos as his main tool, if he can get
the career-focused Rick Manning and the easygoing teacher Isabelle
Winters back together, he just might prove that dog is a *couple's*
best friend....

#1807 IN GOOD COMPANY—Teresa Southwick
Buy-a-Guy
A newly svelte Molly Preston has something to prove. And
"buying" former big man on campus Des O'Donnell as her date
for their high school reunion will go a long way toward righting
old wrongs. Or will it? Because not "winning" Des's love now
seems a far greater wrong.

#1808 SNOW WHITE BRIDE—Carol Grace
Fairy-Tale Brides
When Sabrina White runs away from her own wedding and arrives
on his doorstep in a blinding snowstorm, Zach Prescott's seven
nieces and nephews mistake her for Snow White. And though
Zach doesn't believe in fairy tales, this tycoon can't deny his
young charges a happy ending....

#1809 THE MATCHMAKING MACHINE—
Judith McWilliams
Loyal to her fired coworker, Maggie Romer seethes for revenge
upon the new boss, Richard Worthington. Writing a computer
program that analyzes Richard's preference in women, Maggie
wants to become her, seduce him and dump him! That is, until his
kisses show her that sometimes the best-laid plans of women and
machines can go deliciously awry!

SRCNM0206